Chandi and the Moonstone

A Shattered Moon Novel

Suzi Yee

Text Copyright © 2019 by Suzi Yee

Published by Expeditious Retreat Press
Cover by Vivid Covers
Edited by Elizabeth VanZwolle

For information regarding Suzi Yee's novels and to subscribe to her mailing list, see her website at https://www.joseph-browning.com

To follow Suzi on Twitter: https://twitter.com/Joseph_Browning

To follow Suzi on Facebook: https://www.facebook.com/SuziYeeAuthor

To follow Suzi on MeWee: https://mewe.com/i/josephbrowning

By Suzi Yee

SHATTERED MOON NOVELS: CHANDI SERIES
Chandi and the Moonstone
Chandi and the Pearl of Making
Chandi and the Black Diamond

Chapter One

"Chandi, wake up! We're going to be late for morning devotion." Lucy pulled the curtains open and let the morning light flood their room.

The motionless body in the lower bunk groaned, limbs akimbo. "I'm already still; why do I need to go to morning devotion?"

"You know the rules—no morning devotion, no breakfast." Lucy dragged a quick comb through her auburn hair and splashed some water on her freckled face.

"Well, I do like breakfast…" Chandi started moving her body under the blanket.

"Hurry up…I can't be late again. I hate mucking duty."

"Okay, you've convinced me." Chandi rose. Her hazelnut skin soaked in the warmth of the sun's rays as she stretched her long limbs. "More breakfast, less shoveling shit," she grumbled while she changed out of her sleep clothes.

Lucy laughed. "You dork."

The two novices quickly dashed down the corridors, wiping all frivolity from their faces before entering the main hall. The

Church of Parkour took morning devotion very seriously; it was the only time when the entire monastery gathered together to be one in stillness. Even though discipline was at the core of monastic life, coordinating the movements of a hundred and sixty students from eight to eighteen was tantamount to herding cats.

The sweet smoke from the incense unfurled in their nostrils. They hurriedly took seats in the back as the peel of a gong sounded the beginning of meditation. Khiri, Abbess of the Monastery of Unseen Waters, strode to the front and stopped on the raised center dais that allowed her to be seen by those in the back. The bipedal tigress moved with poise and finesse, and her keen eye scanned the prayer hall, catching Lucy and Chandi as they settled in lotus pose. The mother of the stride made a mental note that they were not *technically* late before nodding to the side and triggering a spin of the prayer wheel—its rhythmic beat gave the meditation its pulse.

"Stillness of the body," Khiri spoke as she sat cross-legged upon the dais, tail hanging limp behind her, her palms placed upward on her knees with her third and first digits in opposition. A highpitched ring marked the first deliberative movement of morning devotion. The room settled and assumed like positions.

"Stillness of the eyes," she voiced as her piercing predator pupils dilated, her gaze softened, and her lids fell. A second ding sounded, and the abbess was confident all followed suit.

"Stillness of breath." Khiri inhaled deeply and breathed out the worries of the day ahead. Another ping sang above the collective exhale of the monastery.

Lastly, Khiri commanded, "Stillness of the mind!" There was no sound except the rotating prayer wheel, periodically respun when its momentum petered out. Chandi was never good with this last step, but she could be still enough so no one would notice. She was a born runner, and the only time her mind was really still was when she was moving.

It was always dicey to be the first to break the stillness of morning devotion, but the call of breakfast was always stronger. Given enough time, someone would inevitably shuffle their body, a stomach would growl, or a sentient would clear their throat, granting the rest of hall tacit permission to break their own stillness and proceed to the commissary for food.

The students were divided into small bands to make things more manageable for the teachers, and it was in those clusters they performed their daily tasks, starting with breakfast. Chandi and Lucy grabbed their warm bowls of porridge before taking a seat on their heels. Breakfast wasn't given much time; it was a stepping-stone to the more important tasks, such as morning chores.

Typically, the Church of Parkour had plenty of lay sentients to manage the day-to-day tasks for their monastic communities, but the Monastery of the Unseen Waters was different. Established in the ruins of Watertown in the Kingdom of a Thousand Islands, its existence was nearly unknown to the laity. The few who did know about it thought it was nothing more than one of many training grounds gifted to the church in exchange for tribute.

This relative isolation required a greater amount of self-sufficiency, and there was no end of tasks to keep both pupils and teachers busy. There were fields to till, crops to plant, weed, and harvest, animals to tend and milk, and endless rounds of washing and cooking, weaving and mending. But when fortune allowed, they were assigned chores suitable to their unique abilities, and every student at the Monastery of the Unseen Waters was special—otherwise they wouldn't be there.

That morning, Chandi was called to serve in the infirmary, a chore she much preferred over weeding or laundry. The infirmary was one of the few places were she felt it was permissible to be openly cheerful—to buoy the spirits of the ailing. A sept of pathfinders and tracers running through an unsecured portion of the ruins had encountered an unknown substance, and when the first of them faltered, they all headed to the monastery for care, arriving late last night. Chandi did little more than sit with them, fluff their pillows, and talk with them; her presence alone was enough to clear the toxin from their bodies. That was what drew the church to her village—it had managed to avoid a wave of disease that wiped out all the surrounding villages, and when a runner of the church fell sick, he was brought to Chandi's home and within a few days, he was cured.

It didn't take the Church of Parkour long to realize the young child had a special ability and offered her family and village protection and investment in exchange for Chandi joining the church. Her mother protested, saying she was too young; Chandi was only five when they came to collect her. But her father knew this was his daughter's chance for a better life. The church would clothe her, feed her, care for her, educate her, and teach her to run. What more could he hope for his daughter under the shattered moon?

So here Chandi sat, eleven years later, listening to accounts of the different ruins the members of the sept had run, wistfully dreaming of the day she, too, would run outside the monastery's walls.

*****

Chores passed by quickly as many hands make light work—an adage that just as easily applied to a multi-limbed sentient as it did to the monastery at large beneath the shattered moon. Besides the one hundred and sixty pupils, there were six administrators, two dozen teachers of various disciplines, and any number of visiting scholars and tracers. Everyone at the monastery was expected to contribute, and visitors were often called upon to share their expertise as guest instructors. Scholars were members of the church who no longer ran and instead passed into the mediation of pure thought. Tracers were the elite runners; many of the visiting tracers were former students coming home to roost between assignments.

That day, Chandi and Lucy's group hosted such a visiting scholar during Tenets of Faith, the time when the thinkers pass their knowledge onto the doers. Today's speaker was Brother Gerrold of the Pensives, on sabbatical to finish his latest treatise on the nature of serenity in movement. Chandi, who had been here the longest of all the students, knew the church's axioms by heart. *In movement, there is purpose. Never take the same path. There are no obstacles, only alternate routes. Flow like water over the land. The way is never the same. The body is only as strong as the mind. Only in stillness can we run true. Only in running can we attain perfect stillness.*

The Church of Parkour was founded on the principle that stillness was the way to escape the cycle of reincarnation that bound sentients to the merciless world beneath the shattered moon, and movement was the best path to stillness. The church never purported that it was the *only* path, merely that it was the fastest. While normal sentients might offer themselves in the service of the stride, not all were born to run, and those selected to train at the Monastery of the Unseen Waters were groomed to be the elite among runners. As tracers, they were interjected into septs all over the shattered moon as the church found need of their unique and varied abilities.

Chandi was certain Brother Gerrold had a wealth of

wisdom to share, but his unfortunate lisp continually cropped up—each "s" propelled spittle from the sides of his mouth—and it became harder and harder for her to suppress a smile, which was enough to tip Lucy into stifled giggles. Thankfully, neither broke during the talk itself, but they were the first out the door to lunch, bursting with laughter once they were out of earshot.

Lunch was always the same: pottage. Sometimes the ingredients varied by season, but the warm nourishing gruel was standard fair for their midday meal.

"Who's the new girl?" Chandi asked between spoonfuls of lentils and greens floating in broth. She nudged her head toward the small figure standing alone holding a bowl. If Chandi had to guess, the new girl had to be close to twelve.

Willem looked up from his bowl. "Her? Dunno. She was in the garden this morning during chores, but I didn't talk to her." He looked at Lucy and asked, "What about you?"

"Her name's Sura. That's all I got out of her before I turned around and she was gone."

Hanu joined them; his simian features held an impish smile. "I could have sworn you two were going to break during Brother Gerrold's recitation." He mimicked the theologian's lisp to perfection.

Chandi answered Hanu but kept her eyes on Sura. "I have no idea what you are talking about. I found Brother Gerrold's points most enlightening." She looked rather old to enter as a tenderfoot; the church usually found them younger than ten.

"Did you hear? They are holding pathfinder trials next week," Willem reported between slurps. "I think I have a solid chance of passing this time." His amphibious background was a great boon in scenarios with water, but it didn't much help with vaults and situational awareness, which were his weak areas the last time he'd tested. At eighteen, he was one of the older novices at the monastery.

Lucy chimed in, "I'll give it a shot. I'm tired of running over the same kit. Hey, where are you going?" she called out to Chandi, who rose to her feet and made her way to Sura. "Oh no, she's found another stray. I swear, she spends one morning in the infirmary and she's got to save everyone."

The trio chuckled only because they knew it was true—Chandi found them all and brought them together one by one. Lucy came to the monastery when she was eight and cried silently every night for her first week until Chandi offered to be her roommate eight years ago. When Hanu was relentlessly harassed by one of the older novices about his tail, Chandi knocked the offender off his feet with a well-timed leg sweep. She did one month's scrubbing duty in the kitchen for that, but the abbess—who was also tailed—did not deem further correction necessary after interviewing Chandi. Violence wasn't the way in the Church of Parkour, but it was often the only way under the shattered moon. When Willem failed his first pathfinder trial, Chandi stayed late after practice to work with him on his problem areas and had managed to narrow the gap down to two. They were all Chandi's strays in one way or another, and they didn't much mind if she found another, but they had to give her a hard time about it. It's what friends do.

"Hey, it's Sura, right?" Chandi softened her voice as to not startle her target.

The blonde girl turned around, full bowl still in hand. "How do you know my name?"

"I'm Chandi," she sidestepped the question. "You want to eat lunch with us?" She motioned to her friends behind her. "They look like total doofuses, but they really are nice," she qualified. Sura looked near human and she was definitely older—probably in her teens—but younger than Chandi. Sura looked uncomfortable under her gaze, averting her pale blue eyes from direct contact. "Tell you what, it's an open invitation. Just look for one of us at dinner. You can't miss Hanu—he's the one with the tail." Sura let a small snort escape. "But you should eat quickly. We'll be moving to the training ground any minute."

Sura peered over the lip of her bowl, watched Chandi return to her friends, talking and ribbing each other as they left for outdoors.

Chapter Two

The four instructors claimed their stations and gear in the courtyard before the onslaught of fledgling runners returned from lunch. Brother Lars, a near human with prominent canines, set up the station for the tenderfoots: strictly the basics—running, calisthenics, jumping, and landing. A column of stackable blocks allowed pupils to adjust the height in six-inch increments for gradual advancement while focusing on form.

Sister Dendra, a plant sentient who constantly switched between bipedal and quadrupedal movement, prepared stations for balance and precision jumping. A four-inch-wide wooden beam was the simplest exercise. It started one foot off the ground but could be raised as high as five. More difficult were the two curved metal pipes—one three inches in diameter and another an inch in diameter—that were held aloft by an adjustable metal frame allowing the bars to spin. Dendra had been known to water or grease them to increase the challenge, but they were currently dry. Last was a deflated fire hose between two mobile winches, permitting trainees to determine the distance and the amount of slack in the line. For precision jumping, Dendra had platforms of varying widths upon which students learned to stick their landings.

Brother Netu, a near human covered with black line tattoos, set up stations to practice vertical motion: climbing, swinging, and tic-tacs. His section of the training yard had a series of walls from five to fifteen feet tall; two rows of angled concrete blocks that faced each other, and both parallel and uneven bars. Lastly, Sister Bibi, a five-foot-tall bipedal eastern cottontail, laid out mats and different-dimensioned soft rigid blocks for rolling and vaulting—the easiest of setups for what many considered the hardest exercises.

With everything in place, the instructors braced themselves for the impending burst of energy. As the flood of tenderfoots and novices flooded the courtyard, Lars corralled the younger children and new recruits and began his lesson.

"This is meditation through movement, where you will learn to run and in the running, find stillness. There are three tenets of running." Lars held up his right hand and counted them out on his fingers. "One, strive to improve. Two, run at your own pace. Three, know your limitations." He dropped his hand. "I will also add as a reminder for us all—no showing off. We do not run for glory, praise, admiration, or gain. We run with precision and humility to attain stillness. A boastful mind is not a still mind." He consulted his clipboard. "I'll be assessing all new tenderfoots; those who have already been assessed, proceed to your station."

Sura lined up with the other new kids, head and shoulders above all of them. She looked around the courtyard while she waited, bodies in silent motion. Even the young ones jumping up and down on platforms landed light-footed. The sound of laughter was notably absent, signaling to Sura this was not child's play.

Sura stepped forward when her name was called. "You're a little older than our typical tenderfoot, so we'll need to go through a few more stations for assessment," Lars informed her. "First, I want you to run to the other side of the courtyard and back." Sura took off, pivoted and stopped in front of the clipboard while the instructor made notes. "Okay, line up here and jump as far as you can." She bent down and held her hands out and pushed off, bringing her arms back. As the dust settled, Lars looked quizzically at her. "Have you trained somewhere before?"

Sura shook her head.

"Where did you learn to jump like that?"

Sura pointed to the novices at the precision-jumping station. "That's how they were doing it." Lars made more scribbles on the clipboard.

"Okay, let's see how high you can jump." He dropped his board face down and stacked blocks to two feet high. "Let's start there." And so she proceeded to perform various feats of jumping, balance, strength, flexibility, and stamina until her body ached.

While the young and the new trainees required more guidance and handling, the more experienced novices divided themselves among the stations and doing laps along the interior of the monastery walls once meditation began. Chandi and Lucy peeled from the hoard and took off running; they would have more time with the equipment if they waited for the initial rush to pass through. Meditation through movement was Chandi's favorite time of day, and Lucy knew better than to talk when they ran together—it was one of the things Chandi appreciated about her. When they returned to the courtyard after three laps, only half the number of students remained: the tenderfoots were winding down to return indoors for didactic lessons, and other novices took their turns running the perimeter of the monastery. Chandi started at the balancing station while Lucy moved to the mats amid the calls of instruction.

"Tuck your head under the opposite armpit to protect that shoulder," Bibi commanded Hanu, who was also at the mats. "Go again."

"Bend your knees; keep them supple to absorb the shock," Dendra advised another novice, who was jumping from a three-foot stack of blocks onto a two-inch metal beam. "Too much forward momentum. Keep your arms back to stick the landing. Again."

"You have to push off with your feet *while* pulling toward the wall with your hands," Netu voiced emphatically at the series of walls. "Kick out your hips and plant this part of the foot against the wall." Netu took a knee to better assess foot placement. "Try again."

Lucy placed a large rigid block on its side and began her progression on the monkey vault. She sprinted toward the padded block, planted both hands on its edge, and landed on it with her knees. Once she had successfully hit her mark ten times, she launched herself at it once more, this time pulling her knees up and in to land on her feet. Soon she'd be able to make a Kong Vault—clearing it without her feet touching at all—but first she must master the monkey.

Meanwhile, Chandi pulled the winches of the fire hose farther apart and slackened the line. Dendra caught her setting up in the corner of her eye and threw out her left hand, populating the terrain beneath the hose with an instant mat of burrs—encouragement for the novice to succeed. Chandi had felt the sting of Dendra's burrs enough times to keep her footing on the fluctuant hose; she steadied herself and then briskly walked the line. Once on the other side, she turned around and returned, going again and again to demonstrate her competence. Performing an exercise once did not count as a success; a successful maneuver was only achieved through repetition without injury or exceeding one's limits—as it is written, so it is ran.

*****

Chandi and Lucy found themselves in the barn with two other novices for evening chores: feeding the animals, mucking the stalls, and turning the compost. "I wasn't even late," Lucy muttered under her breath—the Church of Parkour didn't hold truck with complaints and excuses. Chandi hung back, stopping by the herb garden on the way to their rooms to wash up for dinner. She plucked a few sprigs of mint and herbs and slipped them into her pocket for later.

Unlike breakfast and lunch, dinner was afforded more time and space for fellowship. Long tables and benches were brought into the dining area and the entire monastery gathered as a community. The evening stew often contained meat served with bread, and on special days, there might even be dessert, courtesy of the bees and orchards kept within its walls. It was a time when open talking and laughter brooked no disapproval.

Chandi, Lucy, Willem, and Hanu congregated at the table discussing the happenings of the day. The pathfinder trials featured prominently in the conversation. Lucy and Willem had managed to convince Hanu to sign up, but Chandi was still a black box.

When asked, she answered noncommittally, "I still have a week to decide." Her three companions exchanged looks and were none-too-subtle in their nonverbal objection. "What?" Chandi eventually broke the silence.

Hanu made the first observation. "You didn't sign up for

the last trial."

Chandi broke a piece of bread and dipped it in her stew. "I was out on a tribute visit."

"And what about the one before that?" Willem asked.

"I think I hurt my leg during practice the week before," Chandi postulated.

Before Lucy could open her mouth, an exhausted Sura approached the group. "May I join you?"

"Sure, you can squeeze in here." Chandi made space for the tenderfoot, silently praising the forces that be. "This is Lucy, Willem, and Hanu. Everyone, this is Sura." The cordial greetings and smiles meant Chandi was off the hook for now.

"So how was your first meditation through movement?" Chandi queried politely.

"Okay," the girl answered quietly. *Getting anything out of this one is going to be like pulling teeth*, Chandi thought to herself.

"There's a reason they call new trainees tenderfoots," Willem interjected. "It takes time to build up the calluses and strengthen your body for training."

"But you'll get there eventually," Lucy added quickly, throwing eye daggers across the table. "We have all been there and we have all gotten through it. You will, too." Everyone nodded in agreement.

"Hello, who's that?" Lucy shifted her attention to the sentient entering the dining hall—six feet tall, lean, short brown hair, almond-shaped eyes, and just a little point to the ears. Willem and Hanu turned to look, but Chandi had no need.

"Him? He's a tracer passing through. His sept ran into something toxic in the ruins and they made it here before things got bad. You should have seen him earlier today. I was in the infirmary with them this morning, but he must be on the mend if he's feeling well enough to come down for dinner."

Lucy's eyes narrowed. "You got to sit with him while I was weeding the garden?" The incredulity was as thick as the dregs of Chandi's soup.

The novice shrugged her shoulders. "I go where I am needed."

Chapter Three

Brother Bartholomew had settled in for a quiet night with a book when a succinct knock rapped at his door. He set his book aside and lowered his spectacles from his owlish face. He spoke loudly, "Enter."

A familiar wiry form appeared in the doorway, the light from his lantern glinting in her green eyes. "Am I disturbing you, Brother Bartholomew?"

"Ah, Chandi, come in, come in." The elder shifted books off his second chair to space on the edge of his desk. "Close the door and sit down."

Chandi straightened her posture and accepted the seat. She reached around, pulling out a tome tucked into the back of her pants. "I've finished this one and wanted to return it to you." The weathered spine read *Carvo's Annotated Silence and Meditation.*

"Ah, this is a classic." The wizened hands clasped the book with care. "How did you find it?" Uncertain how to answer, the novice's face spoke volumes. "Not the most enlightening reading, I take it?"

"I did not find it altogether helpful, no," Chandi answered truthfully.

A gleam in the resident scholar's eye preceded a smile and short chortle. "I'm glad you feel that way. It's complete drivel." He placed the book back on his overwhelmed bookshelf. "But you have to read it all to separate the wheat from the chaff."

Chandi breathed a sigh of relief; Brother Bartholomew was not someone she wished to disappoint. He was her first and favorite didactic teacher at the monastery; he had taught her how to read and write. "Would you like to select another?" He waved to the sagging rows of books. She rose from her seat for a better look, and Bartholomew sighed. *How quickly they grow.*

"I almost forgot," Chandi exclaimed, producing sprigs of mint, basil, and spearmint from her pocket. "For your evening tisane." Bartholomew accepted the herbs and moved to his laboratory where he put a glass container of water to boil before steeping the leaves. After careful consideration, Chandi pulled out a title, *Practical Application of Forces.* The scholar squinted and nodded in approval. "I dare say you will find this work more useful."

He eased into his chair and took a sip of his tea. "I hear Brother Gerrold is taking his turn to speak to the novices. Have you had the pleasure?" Chandi nodded. "And? How did you find it?"

Chandi chose her words diplomatically. "His points had their merits, but they were a little circuitous for my mind."

Brother Bartholomew guffawed. "That's because he's a Pensive! Pensives aren't happy until they come to a conclusion that is the exact opposite of their original assertion." He set down his tea and leaned forward. "But I know you didn't come just to bring an old bird his herbs and gossip about the traveling scholars. What brings you here, my child?"

"The pathfinder trials are next week…" Chandi spoke. His bushy brows fluttered over his strigiform eyes.

"Have you decided to sign up?"

"Well, that's what I wanted to talk to you about," she explained. "Should I do it?"

He held up a downy hand. "This must be your decision; no one can make it for you." He retracted his limb. "But I would be happy to listen to your deliberation." He picked up his tea. "What are your concerns?"

Chandi folded her hands on her lap. "What if I don't pass?"

Brother Bartholomew nodded his heart-shaped face. "The first tenet of running is to always strive for improvement. If one stays where they are comfortable and can never fail, there is a strong case to be made that one is not striving," he posited prosaically.

The novice lowered her head. "What if I fail and they won't let me run anymore?" The scholar finally comprehended her dilemma. Chandi had a gift—that's how her parents put it. She had never been sick a day in her life, not so much as a cough, cold, or fever—such a blessing any parent would covet. As

Chandi grew and started walking, fewer villagers fell to disease and toxins encountered in the course of daily life under the shattered moon. Women would draw their water and stop by her parent's cottage to chat while Chandi played amongst the jugs, purifying their water. Soon, sentients would bring their ailing family members just to sit next to the child in case their illness wasn't from natural causes.

Therefore, it was natural to take the sick tracer from the Church of Parkour to Chandi. Everyone assumed he was struck by the epidemic spreading through the neighboring villages, but the runner knew differently—it was radiation sickness. Had the runner headed in a different direction, Chandi might have remained in her village as a healer of sorts, but one that could purify those nearby of radiation could not be ignored.

This made her valuable to the church immediately upon entering the church, regardless if she became a pathfinder or better yet, a tracer. Her monthly visits to the king's estate had been a part of the church's tribute to the Kingdom of a Thousand Islands ever since her arrival eleven years ago. As a novice, she was allowed to pursue training, but would she be permitted to continue were she merely a failed pathfinder?

Brother Bartholomew lay a soft hand on her arm. "Chandi, I've known you since you were this high, and even at five, there wasn't a brother or sister of the stride that could keep you from running, jumping, climbing, and vaulting over everything. I can't make promises and predictions about what church officials higher up will decide—I never had the stomach for administration—but I know our faith requires us to flow like water over the land to find the path of least resistance, and I cannot conceive of a world where forcing you to stop running is the path of least resistance." Chandi looked up and the scholar took her hands into his. "I have no doubt you will make a fine thinker in time, but not before you run."

He studied his former pupil; there was still reticence in her eyes. "Is there anything else?"

"What about Lucy? What if I make it and she doesn't?"

He released her hands and leaned back into his chair, pulling out his pipe and pouch. He struck a match and encouraged the flame to take before extinguishing the light. "If you were to discover that Miss Montenegro had failed to run at her own pace due to the devotion she had for you, would you be pleased?"

Chandi shook her head.

"Do you consider yourself nobler of heart than she?"

"Lucy would make the moon whole if she could."

"Then do her the kindness of treating her as the honorable sister that she is," Brother Bartholomew concluded. "It is getting late and morning devotion waits for no one. If there is nothing more…"

Chandi rose, tucking her new reading into her back waistband. "I'm leaving for the king's estate tomorrow. Is there anything you want me to bring back?"

The owl puffed rings of smoke as he considered. "Does he still employ that marvelous cook that makes the lavender shortbread?"

"Chef Pasleur? I believe she still runs the kitchen."

"If she insists on stuffing your pockets with some of those confections for the road home, I wouldn't mind one or two. They are a bit of all right."

"May you find stillness in the night," Chandi addressed Brother Bartholomew on her way out.

"And to you, my child—and Chandi!" he added abruptly. Chandi turned over one shoulder. "Not a Pensive," he said softly with a wink.

Chapter Four

The captain of the guard rose early to prepare for the monthly journey to the king's estate. It was a day's travel over relatively safe terrain, but the penetrating gaze of the abbess kept Aren on his toes, metaphorically speaking—descended from mountain goat stock, his hoofed feet were no less on edge.

While the theologians in the Church of Parkour were resolute that there is no stillness in violence, the administrators understood the usefulness of having access to protection beneath the shattered moon. In such accord, the Order of the Guard was created. While not technically ordained in the faith, the order was affiliated to and in the service of the church. Once the theologians saw the practical benefits of such an arrangement, their compromise went something like this: not everyone could run, but should that stop them from serving the church in hopes of being reincarnated into one that could run in the next life? From that time forth, adjacent to but separate from each Church of Parkour monastery stood a station of the Order of the Guard.

Aren marshaled his soldiers shortly after breakfast. He

oversaw roughly a hundred warriors, all bearing the black and white quadripartite symbol of the Church of Parkour on their chest. However, this morning, five had donned their dress tabard over their armor. "It's that time of the month again," the captain began. "There are three other units on the road shuttling sentients back and forth on longer routes, which means we are running lean until the envoy returns in three days' time. Consult the duty roster for the most recent assignments. Those headed out today, double check the horses, carriage, and kit before you head to the monastery gates. Dismissed."

A heavy pounding on the thick door announced their arrival , and the opening gate presented Khiri, mother of the stride, followed closely by Chandi. Their carriage, pulled by a four-horse team, was the bed of a large truck fitted with car seats and covered with a sedan hood. The guards took position securing the vehicle: one in the carriage sitting opposite their charges, two sitting up front on either side of the driver, and two hanging on to either side of the back of the carriage. All the soldiers were armed with rifles and spears; if other weapons were carried, they were not visible.

Traveling through the ruins was the most dangerous part of the journey, but it was made less so by the work of the order, which regularly patrolled to make it a safer place for trainees. Once they were out in the countryside, their spartan church regalia would likely be enough to discourage interference from the local sentients.

Chandi liked to watch the ruins pass—crumbling plascrete, burnt-out buildings, and abandoned towering spires. Where most sentients saw the wreckage of past glories, the novice saw endless possibilities in movement. *Flow like water over the land.*

The horses came to full speed once out of the ruins. The church's flag attached to a pole in the harness between the lead horses billowed against the pastoral backdrop. It was a simple design, composed of a pair of horizontal lines in the upper left and lower right quadrant, a pair of vertical lines in the lower left, and a quadrangle in the upper right. The ripple of the flag was one of her oldest memories, from when a carriage not unlike this one came to collect her from her parents' home. All official church vehicles displayed the flag as a deterrent; would-be highwaymen would think twice before attacking such a target. In an unruly, chaotic world, the Church of Parkour was an institution not to be trifled with.

"How goes your meditation through movement, sister of the stride?" Khiri politely inquired.

"Well, Abbess. Thank you for your interest."

"And which book have you brought for edification?" she asked, knowing the novice's penchant for reading. The two had spent many hours on these monthly visits to the king's estate over the years. Chandi pulled out Practical Application of Forces from her meager travel bag and handed it to the tigress. "Ah, a wonderful read."

"Brother Bartholomew thought so as well," Chandi

affirmed, "as I will be signing up for the pathfinder trial after we return." The novice looked sidelong at her traveling companion for signs of reaction, but the seasoned mother of the stride revealed nothing. Not even a whisker twitched.

Khiri handed the book back to the novice. "If memory serves me correctly, you should find it most enlightening, although it has been years since I read it." Nothing more was said and Chandi dived into the tome. Khiri mused at her ever-curious ward behind her stoic, expressionless face.

The carriage arrived a few hours before sundown at the fortified gates of King Dexter VI's ancestral castle. His family's beneficence granted the church its charter among the ruins of Watertown, and Chandi's monthly visit to the estate was part of the church's tribute.

The household was ably run by the king's steward, Tallis, a slender, five-foot-tall bipedal sentient with light fur, beady eyes, and flat set-back ears that vouched for his weasel lineage. He greeted the abbess with charm. "Welcome, mother and sister of the stride. The king welcomes you to his home."

"We accept the king's hospitality and offer our humble service in tribute," Khiri replied with a semi-bow and a formal nod. Book safely stowed, the novice followed behind the tigress with four of the five of the Order of the Guard close behind.

"I'm sure you are weary from your journey," he started as always, which amused Chandi to no end considering the work done in a typical day at the Monastery of Unseen Waters. "We have readied the customary rooms for you and your escorts," he referring euphemistically to the armed and armored soldiers. "Chef has prepared an early meal."

The abbess tipped her head down once more to the steward. Although he was in charge of the king's grounds, his confidence wavered in the presence of the seven-foot tigress.

"However, I regret to inform you that the king has been called away and cannot greet you himself, but he has permitted me to show you every consideration, as is our custom."

"How unfortunate. I do enjoy our little talks," Khiri articulated without a hint of chagrin. She turned to her charge. "Shall we avail ourselves to the chef's piquant handiwork?" The novice nodded obediently, following her lead. Chandi was only five-foot-seven herself, but she felt taller just walking beside the abbess.

The household servants deposited their meager luggage in their rooms while the pair was drawn in by the savory and sweet smells wafting from the kitchen. "Thin as a rail—do they even feed you?" Claudette exclaimed when Chandi entered the kitchen, embracing the girl up and down.

"I assure you she eats plenty, Chef Pasleur," Khiri answered the rhetorical question.

"No need to put on airs with me when the king's away, Khiri," the free-speaking master of the kitchen chided. It always sounded strange to Chandi to hear someone address the abbess so informally, and with so little ceremony. "Come to the table,

I made steak and kidney pie and a trifle for desert."

Claudette chattered on through dinner about sentients Chandi had only ever heard of from her stories, but the abbess nodded her head thoughtfully. The two women stayed on in the kitchen while Chandi made her excuses and headed to the library.

Many years ago, the king's favorite daughter took ill with the measles and the church obliged, sending Chandi to sit with her and purify the disease from her. To pass the time, Chandi read to her from her favorite book, *The Tale of Peter Rabbit*. Once the princess recovered, King Dexter VI was so pleased that he granted Chandi access to his library during her visits, so long as the books were undamaged and returned where they were found.

While Chandi had access to all manner of theological titles from Brother Bartholomew, the king's library was her gateway to secular knowledge. Soon she was surrounded by wall-to-wall bookshelves of histories, atlases, biographies, stories, plays, poetry, and endless treatises on all manner of subjects: mathematics, natural history, astrology, philosophy, and more. The collection was extensive and while there were contemporary works, many dated back to before the moon shattered, scavenged from ruins and traded until they found their home here.

Judging by the thick layer of dust that lay on some of the books, King Dexter VI spent little time here and most of his time in what he called his war room, a study where he plotted with his lords and vassals to expand his kingdom. Chandi could scarcely remember a time the king wasn't at war with someone, and she had been visiting for over a decade. She raised her lantern to the columns of spines and selected her first title.

*****

Chandi had little control over her power to cleanse an area—it was simply on all the time—therefore her role in tribute involved little more than taking a leisurely stroll around the grounds, visiting sick animals and sentients, reading a book by the wells, and holding her nose by the privies. As she was the church's ward, someone from the church had to accompany her, granting them a few days of non-monastic life each month as well. Khiri volunteered for the assignment, leaving the Monastery of Unseen Waters in the capable hands of her prioress Ariadne, an indomitable matron with spider ancestry—she literally had eyes on the back of her head and more than enough limbs to get the job done. Khiri convinced the church elders that sending the abbess to pay tribute would both flatter the monarch and strengthen the church's ties to their benefactor.

Over the years, Khiri had ingratiated her way into the household, winning the favor of the chef and the ear of the king, much to the displeasure of Tallis—he didn't trust any sentient from such a predatory stock. He was right to be suspicious, albeit for incorrect reasons, as the tigress had also been collecting intelligence on King Dexter VI's disastrous wars—hostilities that had reduced the kingdom to two-thirds of its size during his twelve-year reign.

And so the monthly ritual proceeded: Chandi walked the grounds and read voraciously, Khiri eased her way past the locked door and oiled hinges of the absent king's study, and Claudette baked a fresh batch of lavender shortbread for the mother and sister of the stride to carry back to their monastery the following day.

Chapter Five

In the stillness of the night, Chandi stretched out her limbs on the ground, cool now that the warmth of the day had left. The monastery was dark and quiet, allowing all the luster of the stars and the full moon to fill the sky. Chandi often wondered what fractured the lunar body. She found a picture of the moon before the world broke in one of the king's books years ago and marveled at its marbled swirls and perfectly circular shape. There was something called the dark side of the moon—perhaps it destroyed its other half out of spite?

She heard a soft crunch come from behind where she lay. It had followed her from the monastery, but when she turned back, there was no one there.

"Your walk-in-shadows is impressive, but you are going to have to work on the soft step, Sura," Chandi spoke into the night. The blonde tenderfoot blinked into Chandi's peripheral vision.

"How did you know it was me?"

"Call it a hunch," Chandi answered as she patted the ground next to her. Sura accepted her invitation and settled down beside her.

After a spell, the quiet tenderfoot finally broke the silence. "What are you doing out here?"

Chandi smiled—she'd finally figured out how to get Sura to speak. "To watch the full moon."

"Oh," she sounded surprised but looked up at the stars nonetheless. "Can I ask you a question?"

"I believe you just did," Chandi gently ribbed the girl. "Just kidding, of course."

Sura turned her head. "Why did you come up to me my first day?"

Chandi shrugged. "You looked a little lost, like you needed a friend."

"And that's it," Sura voiced suspiciously.

"Not entirely," the novice admitted. "I was curious. Twelve is awfully—"

"I'm thirteen."

"Thirteen is awfully old for a new initiate and I was curious about your gifts," Chandi finished her sentence.

"So everyone has a special power?"

"Everyone here, yes."

"What's yours?" Sura asked timidly, uncertain if it was an altogether polite question.

"I don't succumb to disease or toxins, and in time, I can cleanse an area of such things," Chandi put it plainly.

"So that's why you sit in the infirmary!" Sura blurted loudly before catching herself in mid-sentence.

Chandi quietly laughed. "Yeah, not everyone gets out of outdoor chores so easily." She turned to Sura. "And what about you? I'm pretty good at seeing in low light and I didn't catch sight of you at all. No offense, but there is no way your walk-in-shadows is better than my vision in the moonlight."

Sura took a deep breath before starting, "I can make sentients not see me, when I want."

"That's pretty awesome," Chandi praised both her ability and her disclosure.

"It doesn't work on animals or monsters, but sometimes sentients can be just as bad," she muttered with a tinge of sadness.

"Well, it is certainly useful to a runner," Chandi noted.

"I can do something else," Sura whispered tentatively.

"Oh?" Chandi replied neutrally, trying not to scare off more conversation.

Sura placed a soft touch on Chandi's arm, and Chandi heard in her mind: *Can you hear me?*

Chandi jumped a little. "You're telepathic?"

For a short time and only with those I have touched. You can talk back to me, too. Just think what you want to say. Sura's voice in her head was the same as her spoken voice, only louder.

Chandi furrowed her brow. *Am I doing it?*

Sura laughed. *Yes. And you don't have to try so hard. You only have to think it like you are saying it to me, and I'll hear it.*

This is so cool. How far apart can we be and still talk?

I once got clear across the other side of the village talking to my sis… Sura's voice cut off in Chandi's head and all was silent. Chandi tried think-talking Sura's name, but the girl didn't answer—the connection was broken.

"I have a sister, too, but I've never met her," Chandi offered the silently crying girl beside her. "She was born a few years after I left."

"How did you get word?" Sura wiped her tears. Unlike other monasteries, ties to your former life were strongly prohibited when you entered the Monastery of Unseen Waters, not that Sura had to worry about that—everyone she had was already gone.

"A tracer passing through the monastery was running the ruins not far from my village. Somehow, my mother convinced him to pass the word along." Indra was a formidable woman when she wanted to be, but Chandi mostly remembered her smile and her stories.

"They wanted me before," Sura abruptly changed the subject. "The church. When I was about eight, but my parents refused. Then the raiders came six months ago—razed the village to the ground. My mother told me and my sister to hide, but she isn't…wasn't like me, so they found her but not me. Two days later, a church emissary found me, and once I told them my name, they sent me here."

Raiders? How far did she travel to get here? Chandi thought to herself.

"I figured it didn't matter where the church sent me since I didn't have anyone to keep in touch with anymore," Sura concluded.

"And now, you have us."

*****

Deep in the cosmos, a cluster of rubble circled around the moon, its former pieces now satellites for the remaining bulk of the lunar mass. Caught in the endless circuit around the dross of what was once the lunar colony, disembodied voices wailed their anguish and lamentations. While heard by none, it caused a quiver, like a taut string when plucked. The vibration escalated into wobble, and a chunk of rock fell slightly out of orbit. Had it gone the other direction, it would have crashed back into the moon, adding one more crater to its pock-mocked face, but it didn't. The voices clamored at a near-fever pitch as it soared through the vacuum of space. It entered the earth's atmosphere, the fire burning away its periphery and heating its core. A legion of voices talking over each other all proclaimed the same sentiment.

I'm coming home.

*****

Sura was exhausted, both physically and emotionally. She hadn't told anyone about what happened, and like lancing a boil, releasing the pressure of a held secret helped ease the pain a little. She made her excuses and bid Chandi a good night—she was still struggling with the formal greetings the Church of Parkour was so fond of using. She left Chandi staring at the moon and returned to the comfort of her bed. Even though she had been here a short while, she knew morning devotion waits for no one.

Chandi still hadn't decided what to do about the upcoming pathfinder trials. They were only a few days away, and sign up would be closing soon. The abbess gave no sign of displeasure when Chandi mentioned it, but that didn't necessarily mean anything—Khiri rarely let anything slip. The novice looked up at the stars and the moon, praying for a sign and as if on cue, a shooting star flared in the sky. At least, Chandi thought it was a shooting star until its shine became brighter—it was heading her way.

Chandi leapt to her feet and kept her eyes on the fire in the sky. It came in at a forty-five degree angle, clearing the twenty-foot-tall wall before landing on the far corner of the opposite wall, still within the monastery's grounds. The novice ran to the site, arriving to ribbons of smoke dissipating from a small shallow crater. In the center of the pit lay a small stone, roughly four centimeters in diameter. It glowed in the light of the full moon.

Chandi approached the depression with caution, placing her hand the ground, testing it for heat. The earth was warm, but the air above the stone was tepid. She used the edge of her sleeve to cover her hand and quickly touched it. When a sting of heat failed to register, Chandi tentatively made contact with her bare skin. The meteor was smooth and cool to the touch, retaining a shimmer in the moonlight. Chandi covered it with her other hand and the rock lost its luminance.

Chandi heard the clinking armor of the perimeter guard from the other side of the wall. "All clear," he yelled to his patrol partner toward the front of the monastery. Chandi kicked dirt into the depression and slipped the rock into her pocket before silently footing her way back to the monastery. She passed the pathfinder trial sign-up sheet in the hall on the way to her room and grabbed the short pencil. Below the last name on the list, the novice wrote "Chandini Choudary."

Chapter Six

To put it simply, something broke in science when the moon fractured; as things stopped working, science couldn't fix them and over time, sentients learned to subside on lower tech. Then came the tinkers: sentients infested with nanites that were not only able to repair the technological wonders of the past, but also able to forge new advanced creations from the remains of the ancients' tech that would be inconceivable within the old parameters of reasonable science. In its infinite wisdom, the Church of Parkour employed a cadre of tinkers to keep their technology working, and the magnum opus of their efforts was the adaptive training ground. The metal, plascrete, and rock features in the area were adjustable, thanks to lifts, hydraulics, and more than a little super science. Instructors could raise and lower structures, insert curves and change their concavity, reorient objects, alter angles, and manipulate grades—it was a fully customizable modular marvel designed to polish pathfinders and turn them into tracers. Sometimes called the managed simulation zone, it was also where the pathfinder trials took place.

The lack of stillness in the air was palpable as the twenty novices waited in the courtyard for the trial to begin. Chandi tried everything: deep breathing, the mantra of serenity, visualizing stillness, directing the tide of energy. Despite her best efforts, her pulse quickened, her mind raced, and there was sweat precipitating from far too many parts of her body.

The days preceding were of little help. Once Chandi officially signed up, it was all their group talked about at meals; poor Sura was subject to the minutia of what the pathfinder trials were like, but she found the chatter of her new friends comforting and endured it. Willem, on the other hand, had no peace as everyone sought his experience on the challenge ahead. Failing the trials twice before had been a sore spot for him, and he was pleasantly surprised it was now giving him a certain cachet—which tested the principle of humility central to the church's teachings, but Willem didn't seem too bothered.

The majority of runners trained in traditional monasteries, and were assigned to a sept for ruin running once initiated as a pathfinder. For most runners, being a pathfinder was as good as it got; however, pathfinders trained at the Monastery of Unseen Waters could progress to being tracers of the true path. Tracers were the elite runners, assigned to different septs as their abilities and the church's needs aligned, which was why the novices were so nervous—this was the beginning or end of everything. Once you became a pathfinder and completed your training, you could run the ruins. Once you became a pathfinder, you could continue your training and chart your course to becoming a tracer.

The trials started shortly after breakfast, since the current cohorts of pathfinders that typically trained in the managed simulation zone were running the ruins today and the four instructors who scored the trials needed to train the tenderfoots and novices after lunch. The objective: ten flags in two minutes. Lars, Dendra, Netu, and Bibi observed each applicant's run and scored on a number of factors: number of flags obtained, efficiency of movement, clarity of purpose, planning, and quality of executed maneuvers. The abbess was also present as a tiebreaker, should there be conflict over a novice's score.

The adjudicators entered the managed simulation zone while a few sentients remained in the courtyard to manage the applicants. Chandi recognized a familiar face as a tracer stepped on a ledge. A closer look at his triangular ears, almond eyes, and thin pupils hinted at a vulpine lineage. Chandi could have sworn he had left the monastery with his sept while she was at the king's estate, yet here he was, staring at the huddle of novices with his violet eyes. *Did he always have purple eyes?* she wondered.

He cleared his throat to gather everyone's attention and read from a sheet of paper. "When I call your name, you will enter the testing ground alone. There are ten flags in place. Once you cross the threshold, your two minutes will start. It is up to each applicant to allot their time between thought and movement. A buzzer will sound when you have one minute remaining, again at thirty seconds remaining, and the final buzzer when two minutes have passed. The judges retain the right to ask each of the applicants questions regarding their performance on the course. Once you have finished, you will exit to the changing rooms and remain until all applicants have run to ensure the integrity of the trial. Results will be posted by dinner."

The tracer flipped the page and called out the first of the twenty names, "Novice Muller." Willem took a deep breath and stepped forward. Chandi, Lucy, and Hanu wished him good pathing.

"I wonder how they determine the order. It is random, or by age, or in the order in when we signed up?" Lucy spoke more out of nerves than genuine inquiry.

"Let me go find out," Chandi offered, walking over to the ledge and performing a semi-bow. "Pardon me, brother of the stride. May I inquire the order of our runs?" The pair of purple eyes zeroed in on Chandi. He looked for reinforcements, but all were preoccupied tending to other novices.

"I am uncertain if I may give out that information, sister of the stride," he answered noncommittally.

"I understand," Chandi replied formally. "Thank you for your audience." She moved to return to her friends and remarked in passing. "I'm glad you are feeling better."

A glint of acknowledgement flickered across his face.

"You're from the infirmary, right? Chandi, was it?"

"Yes," she confirmed. Chandi was pleasantly surprised he knew her name but embarrassed that she couldn't recall his.

"What's your last name?" he spoke in a low voice.

"Choudary," she whispered back.

He flipped a few pages around. "Looks like you are going last," he replied quietly. In the distance, he spotted Lucy and Hanu who were signaling to Chandi from the other side of the courtyard. "Just as you signed up," he added casually.

"Thank you, brother of the stride." Chandi gave a slightly less-formal nod. "There were so many of you in the infirmary the other day, I didn't catch your name."

"I'm Mika, Mika Lee," he answered with a slight nod. Chandi returned to her friends, her heart and mind stilled a little.

One by one, the novices emptied the courtyard and Chandi sent Lucy and Hanu off to the trial. She was kicking herself for signing up last, but she used the time to center herself for the coming ordeal. Her eyes were closed when she heard her name.

"Novice Choudary," Mika called her name. She rose with purpose. "Good pathing to you." Chandi paused and nodded before passing across the threshold.

She scanned the grounds, roughly a hundred yards square, looking for color and movement to reveal the flags. Once she saw seven out of the ten, she started to move, figuring the rest were hidden from her initial view.

Chandi sprinted and high-jumped onto a platform, grabbing the first flag and dropping it to the ground. She dashed across a metal beam at a low grade spanning a ten-foot chasm and took the second. She then squatted and leapt into the air, clasping a metal rod to swing her body back and forth three times before exploding off the bar to catch the top edge of a wall. She held on tight, swung her hips back and kicked off with the balls of her feet, pulling her body up with her arms to stand on the wall, securing the third flag. From the high vantage point, she found two previously unseen flags and reconfigured her path.

She cat-leaped through the air from one wall to another and scaled up using her feet again, snagging the fourth flag before twisting over the top to drop on the other side. As her body fell, she extended her hands to absorb some of the shock of the ten-foot fall. Tucking her head under her right armpit, she safety-rolled across her left shoulder to her right hip and immediately found her feet.

The first buzzer sounded, signaling one minute had passed, but Chandi paid it no notice as she dashed across the yard and tacked off one side of a corner, bouncing up and off the wall to grab the fifth flag that dangled from a railing. She tucked her hips under and righted her body as she took off in the perpendicular direction. Chandi picked up speed as she approached a four-foot-high concrete wall, planted her right hand on top, kicked her left leg over, and stepped through with her right foot. Her arms reached out for a metal railing as she arched her body under the bar, seizing the sixth flag as she kept moving around a corner that proved to be a blind end.

She spun a triple reverse tic-tac that aimed her in the right direction for another flag when she heard the second buzzer a few seconds later. As she clutched the seventh flag, she had a decision to make. There were three flags left, of which she only knew the location of two—but they were on opposite corners of the yard.

Never run the same path, she thought.

Chandi angled for the part of the grounds she had run the least, attacking the wall in front of her. She planted her right foot, pushed her forward momentum up while bracing herself with her left hand on the wall, and snatched the eighth flag with her right hand before landing back on the ground, bending deep in the hips, knees, and ankles. She had precious seconds left and made for the last known flag. It was a straight sprint as she leapt up and across a masonry wall and bike rail to another wall top. As she collected the ninth flag, the shadow of the illusive tenth flag waved through an open window in the structure next to her. The final buzzer sounded, marking two minutes passed.

Even though her two minutes were spent, Chandi launched herself through the open window and rolled out, coming up off her left thigh, stepping up on her right foot and capturing the final flag.

She hustled back to the judges, who were making notes in their papers. They looked harried; they were well into their third hour of judging and it wasn't even noon.

Lars asked the first question. "You took four seconds before moving. What did you do with that time?"

"I scanned the area for visible flags by color and movement," Chandi answered.

"And how many flags did you see at that time?" Bibi followed up.

"Seven. I had enough information to start and headed for high ground in hopes of locating the unaccounted-for flags."

All four instructors scribbled more notes while Khiri just stared.

"You heard the last buzzer; why did you leap for the last flag?" the abbess asked.

"The objective was ten flags and the instructions never stated that movement must stop after two minutes. I deemed the artificial constraint of time as an obstacle that should be bypassed since I was aware of the final flag's location and nearby it." Chandi replied.

All writing stopped as the instructors looked at each other and then to Khiri. Khiri nodded her head before addressing the novice. "That is all, Novice Choudary. You may proceed." Chandi formally bowed to the panel and took her leave.

As Chandi entered the changing rooms, all the novices took to their feet under the watchful eye of a chaperone whose role was to ensure the applicants did not discuss the trial itself or their individual runs. The dour observer seemed relieved when she announced, "The last pathfinder applicant has run. You may leave the area."

Lucy grabbed Chandi by the arm, followed closely by Willem and Hanu. While the other novices shuffled out, Chandi reconsidered her displeasure about going last—perhaps it was better than testing early and stewing in your own thoughts, unable to discuss the course or your maneuvers with your peers. It was nearly lunch by the time the quartet returned to the monastery, enough time to compare notes before everyone came in for pottage.

"That was…intense," Chandi broke the silence. Her mind was still processing her run while the others had had at least an hour with their thoughts

"Not a bad word. I would have gone with 'brutal,'" Hanu suggested. He was pretty sure he pulled something going for that last flag. They continued to speak in general terms, skirting around the prohibition against referring to specific obstacles, flags, or performed maneuvers.

Lucy finally cracked, "How many flags did you guys manage to grab?" Their eyes swept to and fro; no one else was around.

Willem muttered under his breath, "Seven."

Hanu mumbled, "Six."

Chandi whispered, "Ten, but I'm not sure the last one

counts." All three gaped at her.

"What?" Chandi demanded defensively.

"Ten?" Lucy squeaked, containing her yell to a hushed tone. "I didn't even see ten flags!" Willem and Hanu nodded in agreement.

"Neither did I at first, but once I started moving around the course, I spotted more flags," Chandi explained.

Willem was the first to recover. "That's great, Chandi! Congratulations." He gave her a semi-bow. Chandi blushed, unaccustomed to praise—she didn't run for glory, but it was nice when others noticed.

"What about you, Lucy?" Chandi queried, eager to shift attention away from herself.

Lucy bit off her words brusquely, "I don't want to talk about it."

"Everyone only remembers their missteps, Lucy. I'm sure it's not that bad," Hanu attempted to mitigate her embarrassment. The kitchen staff was starting to put out bowls for the forthcoming pots of pottage.

"Trust me, it didn't go well," Lucy affirmed. Chandi wanted to respect her friend's wishes, but now she really wanted to know. *How bad could it be?*

"We all shared, and you asked—"

"Four," Lucy spat the number out distastefully. "Are you happy? I only grabbed four." They were momentarily speechless.

"What happened?" Willem inquired gingerly.

"I just froze. I walked in, didn't see ten flags, and I panicked," Lucy explained. "I didn't even start moving until after the first buzzer sounded." The redhead was in near tears.

The rest of the monastery filed in for lunch, and Sura found them squatting in one corner in silence without bowls in their hands. "How did it go?" she asked politely.

"We aren't supposed to talk about it," Willem declared. He rose and stood in line for two bowls of pottage, one for himself, the other for Lucy. Sura scanned each of their faces and understood—now was not the time for words. They proceeded to eat lunch in silence—even Hanu didn't crack any jokes or remarks—before making their way to the courtyard for meditation.

Chapter Seven

"As you know, pathfinder trials took place this morning." Dendra addressed the courtyard before the students dispersed to their stations. "Results will be posted by dinnertime. Do NOT ask us about scores or performances. All inquiries will end in an abrupt dismissal from meditation and double evening chores. If any of this morning's applicants feel they may have sustained an injury that interferes with their meditation, see Lars for assessment immediately."

Chandi and Lucy took off running in silence, but the quiet felt strained and tense rather than still. When they returned to the courtyard after their three laps, there were fewer novices at the stations than normal; Chandi guessed more than a few were nursing injuries. Everyone scattered to evening chores, waiting for dinner to come. There was only so long one could anguish, and the emotionally exhausted just wanted to know one way or the other.

The results were posted in the same spot as the sign-up sheet, each applicant's name in careful scrawl followed up a single word: "pass" or "fail." There were no rankings, scores, or number of flags noted—such things strained humbleness and invited hubris in the church's mind. Willem and Chandi passed along with six other novices. Hanu and Lucy did not.

Lucy disappeared after dinner, and Chandi grew worried when she hadn't returned by evening reflection. Chandi pulled out the loose brick in the wall just below her bed frame and removed a piece of shortbread. Chandi checked the cache for her other stashed items—a necklace with a lotus pendent and the meteor, which she had taken as a talisman of sorts. Had it fallen on any other night, she wouldn't have even been there. As it was delivered from the cosmos during the full moon, she'd taken to calling it "Moonstone" in her head. Chandi wrapped the confection in linen, tucked it into her pocket, and left to find Lucy.

*****

The murmurs of the meteor grumbled with discontent. It had been days since they'd landed back to Earth, but none who'd crossed the veil made it to the other side. Were they not home? How long had they waited, only to find an abyss between them and the other side? The clamor of voices fell on deaf ears.

Where is the land beyond the veil?!

The chasm is too wide!

But we are home—fate has robbed us again!

Find another path!

All paths lead to oblivion!

The din died down as the days passed. Some embraced nonexistence over waiting, others scoured the terrain of the otherworld for another point of entry. But the determined and the desperate remained, watching the chasm just beyond the veil.

*****

There was a tap at Willem's door, the second of the night. Willem found Chandi on the other side.

"Is Lucy here?" she spoke just loud enough for anyone inside to hear. "I come with a peace offering."

Willem stood in the doorway, unsure how to answer. A sniffle came from inside.

"What is it?" Lucy whimpered.

"A cookie."

"One of the fancy ones from the king's cook?"

"She prefers to be called 'chef,' but yes."

There was a palpable pause before Lucy spoke. "Can you give us a minute, Willem?"

Willem considered pointing out that this was his room, but he reconsidered the wisdom of that path. He opened the door, letting Chandi pass before taking his leave.

Lucy was sitting on the made bed, her nose snotty and her

eyes puffy and red. The single bed seemed too small for the gulf between them, so Chandi squatted on her heels beside it.

"I'm sorry," Chandi whispered.

"For what?"

"For how the trial went and making you talk about it."

"I'm not mad at you," Lucy clarified. "I'm glad you passed and I would have kicked your butt if you dodged another trial." She wrung out a well-used handkerchief. "I'm mad at myself for panicking—once I started moving, I was fine. I'm mad that things have to change." She blew her nose. "I thought you said you brought a cookie."

Chandi rose and took a seat on the bed, placing the square of shortbread between them. Chandi knew Lucy was right—things were going to change. They wouldn't meditate together anymore once Chandi started morning training with the pathfinders. They would make new friends and memories that didn't de facto include each other.

"You want to hear the latest news?" Chandi knew which side Lucy's bread was buttered. Lucy nodded and tore off the corner of her cookie. "Among the novices that passed, the fewest number of flags collected was six."

"Really?"

"Really," Chandi confirmed. Lucy took a bigger bite into the crumbling sweetness.

"How did you get the others to talk?"

"I have my ways," Chandi voiced mysteriously. Lucy almost

laughed.

"Wait—if six was good enough, why didn't Hanu pass?"

"He injured himself. If you can't do the maneuver without injury, if counts as a fail. *Know your limitations*," Chandi quoted the tenets.

"Listen, I only got four flags my first fifty-six seconds, so it's not like you *aren't* a good runner," Chandi argued. "You said yourself you were fine once you were moving. You have six months before the next trial and if Willem can pass, so can you." Lucy loosed a snort and a chortle; Chandi hadn't intended to throw him before the proverbial crocophant, but she'd take the win.

"We'll never see each other," Lucy sighed.

"I'm still your roommate, remember?" Chandi pointed out. "And we can have dinner together—last time I checked, pathfinders still eat dinner."

"Won't you want to hang out with your new pathfinder friends?" Lucy baited her friend.

"Did you see the list of novices that passed? None of them are nearly as companionable as you." Chandi was only half joking. "As far as I am concerned, I'm just scouting ahead for your arrival. We'll meet at dinner so you can inform me of what is happening in the courtyard, and I'll bring news from the training ground."

Lucy nibbled on what was left of her cookie. "What's this flowery taste?"

"It's called lavender. It doesn't grow around here and King Dexter imports it specifically for this recipe."

"I suppose we should give Willem back his room before I cover his bed with crumbs," Lucy capitulated.

"It may be too late for that, but if it is any consolation, I have one last cookie we could split?"

"Deal."

*****

Hanu walked the orchards in the cool evening air, caught in that paroxysmal dilemma of being exhausted but not being able to sleep. He had run the gamut of highs and lows today and stillness eluded him, so he sought solace among the trees. They weren't the same as the ones as back home, but they gave him a place to be arboreal.

He picked a sturdy apple tree to scale and stopped at the first big branch; his calf was still bothering him and he didn't want to risk greater heights. Just as he was about to settle, he heard a sniffle from the other side of the tree.

"Anyone there?" he called out in the night. When no one answered, he made his way to the other side and saw nothing. He passed back to his branch, leaned against the trunk and let his tail swing in the breeze. He heard shuffling from the other side again but didn't bother to investigate. "I know someone's there. You might as well come out."

Hanu waited until he saw Sura's small form climb around to his branch. He moved down to make space for her. "Hi," she shyly greeted him. She wasn't sure where to look as they sat side by side on the limb, but she knew it was rude to stare at his tail.

"Hey," Hanu replied. "You're not bad at climbing trees for someone that isn't a monkey." She looked sideways at him and caught his grin.

"Thanks. I used to climb trees all the time at home…"

"Me too. Well, I actually used to live in trees, so there wasn't really much choice in the matter." Sura stifled a laugh. "Feeling a little homesick?" Hanu guessed.

"Maybe a little," Sura admitted.

"I get it. There are a lot worse places to be under the shattered moon, but this is not home." Hanu shrugged. "Why do you think there were so many applicants at the trials? Becoming a pathfinder is a sure ticket out of here."

"I'm sorry you didn't pass," Sura murmured, dangling her legs in the air.

"Thanks. It's disappointing, but not a complete surprise. I figured it was a long shot—fifteen is pretty young for a pathfinder —but I had to try. How else was I going to know my limitations if I don't push against them from time to time?" Hanu joked as he twisted the tenet and Sura's airy laugh filled the foliage. Hanu smiled; he liked to make sentients laugh— there were tears enough under the shattered moon and someone had to even the score.

"I promise it gets better," Hanu spoke softly. Sura nodded.

"Can I ask you a question?" she changed the subject.

"Sure!" Hanu wasn't used to being a font of knowledge among his peers.

"Your tail—does it work?" Sura asked tentatively. Hanu let loose a hearty chuckle. Her cheeks reddened and she immediately withdrew her question, "I'm sorry, that was rude. It's just…I never met a monkey sentient before."

Hanu composed himself; he was unaccustomed to someone so reserved. "The more polite term is 'simian' but I won't hold that against you, since you've never met one before," he reassured her. "Hold out your arm." Sura offered her forearm and Hanu wrapped his tail around it and squeezed. She sounded a reflexive squeak. "It's not as good as another set of opposable thumbs, but it comes in handy."

Sura giggled at his pun, which was refreshing as his puns were only tolerated by most. As his tail was otherwise preoccupied, he swung his legs in the night air instead.

*****

The abbess was finishing the last of her missives late into the night when a rap fell on her door. Khiri pushed back her fatigue before answering, "Enter."

"Ah, Brother Bartholomew, to what do I owe the pleasure," the tigress commented to the strigiform visage that graced her door.

"A former pupil dropped this off as a gift." The scholar produced a bottle with amber liquid inside. "Remembered I had a penchant for it—purely to facilitate contemplation. I surmised you'd had a long day and thought you might benefit from a glass."

Khiri opened the deep bottom drawer of her desk and produced two glasses. Brother Bartholomew interpreted that as an invitation and closed the door behind him.

"Twenty applicants—that's quite a lot," he posited as he poured. The spicy fruity aroma of the liquor filled the air.

"Largest turn out yet," the abbess confirmed, and accepted a glass.

"I also heard someone collected all ten flags," he offhandedly remarked.

"I don't know where you could have heard that, Bartholomew. The graders and the applicants have strict orders not to discuss the trial, to ensure the integrity of the test." Khiri took a drink and felt the sweet fire go down her throat.

Bartholomew let out a short hoot. "You can't keep something like that from a nosy old bird like me, Khiri."

"I can neither confirm nor deny such chatter." The warmth of the liquor started to spread to her face and limbs.

"If it were true, it's been years since a novice ran so well in a trial," he baited the tigress.

"Except I did it *within* the allotted two minutes," she

corrected the scholar.

His eye were mirthful while he shook his head. "You brought her in—you only have yourself to blame."

"I was merely illuminating a distinction between two seemingly similar phenomena—something an Analytical like yourself would appreciate."

Bartholomew guffawed, his spirit loosened by the brandy. "Between two old friends—tell me, how did she run?"

Khiri sat back in her chair and motioned for a refill. She allowed her countenance a brief respite from its neutral mask. "You should have seen her, Bartholomew. She was magnificent."

Chapter Eight

"There's more to being a pathfinder than runnin'," Bibi began, smoothing the fur down her ears as she paced in front of the ten new initiates. "A pathfinder must be aware of all obstacles to find the most efficient route. A pathfinder must remain silent and hidden in their movement. A pathfinder must learn how to move in a sept." Her slight draw stretched the words out, adding syllables where there were none.

"You have all demonstrated a grasp of the basic meditations, but a pathfinder must internalize the movement in order to synthesize the fluid motion that only flows from a still mind."

Chandi glanced sideways at Willem, who stared intently at the instructor. He had waited a long time for pathfinder orientation and wasn't going to miss a word.

"These first two weeks will be intense training, both in the adaptive training ground and indoor didactic work. During this period, you will be excused from either morning or evening chores, but you will be expected to perform at least one set; everyone contributes to the upkeep of the monastery."

Chandi recognized the other trainees in passing but didn't

know any of them very well save Willem, as they were from other clusters. Jukka was one of the few mutated plants at the monastery. Even though he could take other forms, he assumed a roughly humanoid shaped to be less jarring to the other sentients. Mira and Natalie were the Chandi and Lucy of a different cluster—they did everything together and sat next to each other during orientation. Seeing them huddled and sharing knowing glances made Chandi miss Lucy's presence even more. Joshi was a casual acquaintance of Willem's; even though he was younger than Willem, they had joined the monastery around the same time. Going through tenderfoot training together was one experience that bound them to each other, despite the divergent paths on which they found themselves in subsequent years. Finn, only fifteen, was the youngest initiate in the cohort. He naturally grew brightly colored feathers and he took care to pluck his plumage regularly—his clothing could reduce the shine from his iridescent skin—but the feathers were too long and bright to hide and thus had to be sacrificed.

And then there was Yan. Yan was known for keeping to herself and seemed quite content with that company. She was petite, no more than five-two, but she could run like the wind with lithe grace. Her silky black hair, the peach undertone in her skin, and the epicanthic fold over her slim eyes suggested an Asian ancestry, but Yan wasn't known to share much about herself to anyone during her time at Unseen Waters.

"After two weeks, regular schedules will resume with

meditations in the morning and Applied Tenets of Faith in the afternoon. We will slowly integrate you with the established pathfinders, beginning with highly supervised runs in the nearby ruins." The mention of running outside the monastery walls stirred everyone's interest. "But there will be plenty of time for questions before we embark outside the managed simulation zone. Right now, our focus is to get you all ready by that time." Bibi handed off to Dendra, who held a clipboard in her leafy dendritic hands.

"There was quite a turn out for the pathfinder trials and your cohort is one of the largest to orient, so we will be availing ourselves of a guest instructor, Tracer Lee." Chandi's pulse quickened at the mention of Mika's name. Dendra motioned to the back where Mika gave a formal bow. "Today you start your journey as a pathfinder. Once your training is complete, you may choose to remain a pathfinder and be assigned to a sept. However, it is our hope that all of you will stay, because we know we can make tracers out of all of you. Brothers and sisters of the stride, dismissed."

True to Bibi's word, the next two weeks were grueling. Chandi learned to blend into her surroundings, regardless of light and weather. She gained five different types of silent stepping depending on terrain and intent. She picked up how to communicate with her arms and hands. But her favorite part was the adaptive training ground, which changed features every few days.

The church viewed meditation through movement as a personal endeavor and training was often self-directed with corrective measures from instructors as needed. In the courtyard, novices moved through stations, but as pathfinders, they picked a section of the training ground to move through. As their skills increased, they were expected to increase the challenge.

Always strive to improve.

That meant drops came from greater heights, terrain came at different angles or curves, and pathing through obstacles required a combination of maneuvers. They also started training with loaded packs varying in materials, weight, and distribution to prepare for actual scavenging. Sometimes there were other pathfinders in the area and other times they were running the ruins, leaving the trainees the 100x100 yard simulation zone all to themselves.

Besides individual training, they used the area to start group training. While every runner must run at their own pace, a pathfinder must run as a sept and they were divided into randomized groups of four. They were given a starting point and end destination and instructed to move together as a group. The initial runs were not pretty. The first day, Jukka crawled under a bar that Natalie used to jump off of and one of his thorns planted deep into her foot, Yan vaulted over a wall and broke Finn's momentum on a vertical-jumping sequence, and there were no less than three collisions amongst the eight initiates.

Just as a group started to move together, use hand signals to coordinate, and gather awareness of each other, the instructors would mix the groups up again. Once they were tracers, they wouldn't have the luxury of sept familiarity on a run—tracers went wherever the church needed them, and Dendra wasn't joking when she said they intended to make tracers of them all.

Each sentient's personality was expressed in how they moved through the same terrain: some crawled under things while others went over them; some vaulted while others jumped; some climbed while others tic-tacked; some rolled over their right shoulder while others rolled over their left; some were better at quadrupedal movement, while others had little regard for spatial orientation at all. Chandi had only ever mediated with Lucy on a regular basis and her rhythm had become second nature to Chandi—having to accommodate other sentients' styles and cadences was very much another obstacle to path around.

Once the pathfinder initiates grasped the basics of moving as one, Netu released his scritch Umbra to test their stealth. The black lines and patterns on his skin that looked to be no more than tattoos leeched from his body and took the form of a giant black tarantula, each of its eight legs up to two feet long. Its fuzzy body was covered in short urticating hairs and its poisonous spit was enough to make Chandi a little queasy, a biofeedback she experienced when something highly toxic was nearby. Bonded to Netu, Umbra took basic instructions so the pathfinders were in no real danger, but the scritch was a living thing with a penchant for hunting. Umbra's keen senses sussed out their early attempts at stealth, but as the days progressed, the pet arachnid was just another obstacle to be circumvented.

The last few days of the crash course were assigned to individual meditation in preparation for their first run in the actual ruins. Chandi found herself pitted against a stubborn corner where two ten-foot-tall walls met. She knew she could jump and climb it, but she wanted to tic-tac—a maneuver that would allow her to scale higher obstacles than a simple climb and pull-up would. No matter how many times Chandi tried, she could only get two vertical steps before losing momentum, and the otherwise even-keeled pathfinder was about to hurl something at the nook that eluded her. She grunted her displeasure and mustered her determination, running full speed at the right wall once more, taking two steps on the walls before landing back on the ground in failure.

"You're hitting too high on the wall," Mika commented from behind her. Chandi turned around—in her frustration, she'd let him sneak up on her. *Thank goodness this isn't a ruin and he wasn't a horc*, Chandi thought to herself.

"Come to the wall," Mika motioned to her. "Your angle of entry and speed are good, but your foot is hitting here." Mika placed his hand on the wall. "Which is fine if you're six feet tall, but for your height, you need to be hitting more like here," he suggested, and moved his hand lower down the wall. "Try planting your foot here so I can check the angle."

Chandi raised her right leg and placed the ball of her right foot where Mika indicated. He looked from different viewpoints, making slight adjustments. "Now flex your right ankle, knee, and hip, and push off," Mika advised.

Chandi complied and sprung off the wall, nearly colliding with Mika from the unexpected force. The tracer deftly moved to the side and caught the flying pathfinder. "See the difference in power?" he asked with just a hint of humor in his eyes.

Chandi found her feet and extricated herself from his arms. "I see what you mean." she replied sheepishly.

Mika chuckled. "Don't worry, it happens to all of us, especially as one grows taller. We all have to make adjustments from time to time. Your secret is safe with me," he spoke in a semi-conspiratorial tone. "Once you know how to generate the force, you just have to work on directing it up." He nodded to Chandi's nemesis. He looked beyond to another section of the simulation zone and yelled, "Use your arms to guide your maneuver and reduce your impact!"

He turned back to Chandi. "I better go check on the pathfinders working on their high drops before someone dislocates a shoulder or breaks a collarbone," Mika excused himself with a slight bow. Chandi returned the gesture before setting up for another run at the corner. "And Chandi, be sure to practice approaching from the other side. I know you're stronger on your right, but you are not always going to be able to tackle all obstacles from the right side." He gave her a smile before dashing off.

*****

"Everything hurts," Willem groaned as he cautiously took a seat at dinner. Chandi nodded in agreement—it seemed like every day she found a new bruise or ache, sometimes every hour. "Nobody told me being a pathfinder was going to hurt this much. Dendra had me crawling on all fours over and under the training ground today." Willem rubbed his sore elbows and shins.

"I battled with a ten-foot wall intersection," Chandi replied as a sign of solidarity.

"Who won?" Hanu asked as he took a seat.

"It's a draw," Chandi admitted, "for now."

"What's a draw?" Lucy interjected as she and Sura sat at the table with their bread and stew.

"Whether it was a good idea when we signed up for the pathfinder trials," Chandi joked.

Lucy shook her head. "You two don't fool me—you're loving every second of it."

"It's fine in the doing," Willem conceded. "It's the achy aftermath I could do without."

Sura's quiet but precise voice piped up, "A brother of the

stride once told me that it takes time to strengthen the body for training." Willem ate his own words with his stew while the others snickered.

"I wouldn't listen to that guy. Word is he's unreliable," Hanu added.

"How are things going in the courtyard?" Chandi artfully changed the subject.

"I finally nailed the monkey vault and now I'm working on the Kong," Lucy replied.

"My calf feels a lot better and I'm back to full practice," Hanu reported. "Apparently, I'm 'landin' too heavy on my heels,'" Hanu mimicked Bibi's characteristic draw.

"How's tenderfooting?" Chandi directed her question to the reserved blonde tearing at her bread.

Sura wobbled her head ambivalently. "Brother Lars thinks I might be ready to advance to novice in two months' time."

The table paused. "Really?" Chandi managed to eek out.

Sura picked up on the collective vibe. "Is that good? Or bad?"

"That's great!" Lucy exclaimed. "Most trainees spend at least a year as a tenderfoot."

Sura continued, "Brother Lars says because I'm older, my body is stronger and with dedicated practice, I could advance faster than the average tenderfoot. He and Sister Dendra have been working on my stamina—I can only run one lap around the monastery perimeter."

"Don't feel bad—one lap's five kilometers!" Hanu reassured her. Sura shrugged, having no concept of how far that was—it felt like miles—and it was longer than she cared to run after lunch on some days.

"Honestly, I'll be glad to be training with sentients my own age," Sura replied. For a shy sentient who normally didn't like to stand out, Sura felt very conspicuous as the oldest and tallest tenderfoot.

"What's the news from the training ground?" Lucy inquired.

"We managed to avoid Netu's scritch," Willem proclaimed victoriously.

"Joshi got called out for doing a wall spin," Chandi offered.

"A what?" Hanu was clearly intrigued.

"Where you plant your palms on a wall and spin three-sixty inverting your body around," Willem elucidated.

Lucy looked confused. "Couldn't you just tack off the wall and end up in the same place?"

"Exactly," Chandi confirmed. "It's just for decoration. It doesn't overcome any obstacles or help keep motion fluid."

"It sounds pretty cool though," Hanu conjectured, picturing it in his mind.

"Just don't let any of the instructors catch you practicing it," Chandi warned him. "You could at least make an argument for palm spins to change direction over railings or terrain with nothing there to tack off of, but there isn't any wiggle room for wall spins."

"Joshi always liked flashy maneuvers." Willem sighed with resignation. "*Everyone must run their own path at their own pace.*"

Chapter Nine

Jackson donned his cargo vest, checking each pocket for his required kit. He elected for trousers over robes for better maneuverability. After rubbing his belt buckle until it shined, he fastened his sheathed foot-long dagger around his hip.

He geared up more out of habit than anything else; the ruins around the Monastery of Unseen Waters were thoroughly picked and fairly clean of spirit activity, not to mention the monastery itself. Jackson couldn't remember the last time the abbess required him to take care of a spirit during his eight-year tenure. His job was largely applying the church's sigil on its trainees and making sure the nearby ruins were safe for training pathfinders, leaving him ample time to craft his own spells.

Not that it stopped the voices.

Ever since Jackson could remember, the voices of the otherworld murmured in his ears. No one else could hear them, just sorcerers, those of the stock before the moon shattered. It was enough to drive a person mad, were they not a constant companion from birth—utterances of past sorcerers offering up their knowledge and spells, cries of the dead, and sounds of the beings that dwelt on the other side of the veil.

At first glance, a sentient might think sorcerers and the Church of Parkour were incompatible. How could one who heard the mutterings from the otherworld have a still mind? A sorcerer would tell you that in order to use magic, one has to find the silence within to channel the energy, which was not completely incongruous with church doctrine. The church theologians would argue that sorcerers—humans unchanged by the forces that granted other sentients abilities under the shattered moon—are the most in need of escape from the cycle of reincarnation. The church administrators would point out the relative rarity of sorcerers and the utility of magic, not just in daily tasks but in protection from supernatural activity.

While minor spirits interfered in subtle ways, there were far more malevolent and angry beings that lived in the otherworld, waiting for their chance to pierce the veil between worlds and be made flesh under the shattered moon. Sorcerers could sense spirits while still in their ghostly otherworld form, gather information from other spirits and dead sorcerers to identify them, and once defeated, bind the vanquished spirits-made-flesh into physical items where they could be used to enchant things or simply prevent them from being made flesh again.

Thus in the Council of Bellevue, the church elders adopted a tolerant, utilitarian stance on sorcerers. Unlike warriors, they could serve in the church and were allowed to find stillness in running the otherworld rather than the world under the shattered moon. That decision decades ago was the reason Jackson's room was inside the monastery walls next to the resident scholars instead of outside with the Order of the Guard, not that it mattered once they got out to the ruins.

The sun was bright in the sky by the time Jackson made it to the keep and joined the squad. Their clanking armor reflected the light in different directions as they headed into the untamed portions of Watertown; Jackson pulled his wide-brimmed hat down to keep the glare out of his eyes. He and a squad of ten soldiers made their rounds in the ruins regularly on days when no pathfinders were scheduled to run, looking for changes or new dangers. No matter how many times they combed the ancient city's remains, there was always the possibility of hazards—ruins under the shattered moon regenerated. Some changed rapidly, but even a low-frequency ruin like Watertown could produce new creatures, items, or buildings.

The path is never the same.

Their task was straightforward—the soldiers looked for changes in the landscape and scanned for mundane risks while Jackson checked the otherworld. They were almost finished with their sweep when Jackson heard a rumbling coming from the other side of the veil.

"Look alive—we've got something coming through!" Jackson yelled as he grabbed his dagger in one hand and reached into his upper right pocket with the other. He cleared his thoughts and found the silence within amid the din of voices only he could hear. He started chanting in a tongue only sorcerers seemed to know, and the Order of the Guard knew what it meant even if they didn't know what Jackson was saying—a ghost was coming through.

The sorcerer spoke with rhythmic fervor as the warriors took defensive stances. They didn't know what was coming or where it would appear, but they had their weapons ready. A cold wind moved through and the sky seemed to darken despite the bright sun above them. Jackson blew the grains of salt he had fetched from his pocket into the air in front of him and commanded the spirit to show itself.

A roughly humanoid mist blinked into existence, slipping through a rip in the veil between worlds. Its eyes were piercing orbs of red light as it looked side-to-side, gathering its bearings as newly-flesh. The readied guards advanced, spearing the cottony creature in its side and legs without any discernable affect. It opened its mouth and released a vapor that clung in the air. The miasma seeped into their skin, causing a wave of abject despair. Five guards dropped their weapons, fell to the ground, and wailed uncontrollably. One guard drew his short sword, taking aim for his own side, *What's the point?* coursing through his mind

"Altered state," Jackson heard the voices. "Spirit of discord," he picked from the ever-pressing mumblings. The sorcerer once again found the stillness and repeated the words of magic whispered in his ear. He brought his wrists together as he recited the spell and from their union, a gust of wind dispersed the noxious cloud. His intonation rose as he stepped forward and slashed at the mist's form.

A hideous scream pierced the ruins as a black light radiated from Jackson's cut. Once they saw the creature take damage, those soldiers of the Order of the Guard who had kept their wits and weapons started stabbing it with their spears, poking more holes where beams of dark radiance spilled forth. As he raised his dagger and slit the creature's throat, Jackson uttered his last command to the spirit in a language only he and spirit understood: "Come to me."

The mist and dark light swirled into a whirlwind, aimed directly toward Jackson's belt buckle. The gale died down to a breeze once all traces of the spirit disappeared, bound inside the sorcerer's charm. Jackson looked around to check for causalities: the attacking guards held fast to their weapons, the guards on the ground were finding their feet, and the soldier holding the short sword had luckily not made it through his armor.

"Everyone okay?" Jackson queried the group. Grunts and nods were all he got. "Knolls, you're lucky you've still got a liver for the drink I'm going to buy you tonight." A couple of the guards chuckled.

Jackson sheathed his dagger and checked his pockets once more. "Ruins look good to me. Let's go get some lunch."

*****

The rules of the run were simple. Keep up. Don't get injured. Stay unseen and unheard. If you encounter something in the ruins, hide. If you are made by a friendly sentient, a sept leader may open communication with caution, but if it is aggressive or non-sentient, run. Precious few could outrun a pathfinder of the Church of Parkour under the shattered moon. It went without saying, all other tenets of faith and mediation applied.

Scavenging was allowed and the runner was given a percentage of their finds. For large items, they would make note of the location for the Order of the Guard to pick it later, but for small or light treasures, they were equipped with small daypacks strapped tight to their backs. If you broke a rule of the run, you surrendered all your finds from that run.

While church doctrine was adamant that the purpose of running the ruins with efficiency, precision, and humility was to attain stillness, it also acknowledged that the rest of the world beneath the shattered moon relied on accumulation of resources. They argued that even though wealth was not the object of pathing the ruins, their organization and runners would need it to perform their various ministries and meditations.

Willem perked up when Lars reviewed the rules of scavenging; these supervised runs were his chance to build a reserve for when he left the monastery. He was still undecided about whether to stay for tracer training or be assigned to a sept as a pathfinder. Once he left the Monastery of Unseen Waters, he would be allowed to contact his family, and as a practicing pathfinder, he could transfer his wealth to them. Even though they had parted ways eight years before, he still felt responsible for them, especially his five younger siblings. At the time, the church's beneficence for Willem made sense, but now that he was a grown man, the walls of the monastery seemed more a cage or crutch than an opportunity.

Chandi was lost in her own thoughts, as well. She no longer had to watch the ruins pass by her carriage window—she was finally going to run them. Granted, it was only once a week and only for a few miles of the closest, most-traveled ruins of Watertown, but it was a start.

Lars divided the trainees into two groups of four, one led by himself with Bibi in the rear heading south and the other led by Dendra with Netu bringing up the rear going north. Once the monastery gates opened, they took off running.

*****

The many voices of Moonstone no longer spoke as one, broken and scattered in their despair. Some had surrendered to the great beyond while others continued to look for another path. But two small spirits kept their vigil on the veil and the chasm beyond.

Over there! one spoke excitedly.

It is always the same, the second answered flatly, *the chasm behind the veil.*

No, look harder. I can see the other side.

The second spirit squinted. *Maybe that was land ahead? But it is still so far away.*

But it's closer! the first sprit exclaimed. *If it can get closer, the abyss isn't unchanging. Perhaps the chasm can close.*

The second spirit was no great thinker…but if it had waited this long, why not wait a little longer?

Chapter Ten

The rhythmic click of the carriage wheel marked time as Khiri and Chandi made for the king's estate once more. The ruins seemed different to Chandi now that she'd run in them. They seemed smaller somehow, less unknown and unknowable. Even the tall spires seemed less formidable. She wondered how they looked to the abbess.

Chandi leaned back into her seat, glad for the rest after an intense two weeks of orientation. Once she returned from the king's estate, normal training schedules would begin and she was grateful for the reprieve. Khiri noted the pathfinder's lack of interest in the passing ruins; typically, she would be glued to the window until the view transitioned to the countryside. Chandi hadn't even pulled out a book.

"How goes your meditations, sister of the stride?" Khiri asked evenly.

"Well, Abbess. Thank you for your interest," Chandi replied mechanically. She was too tired not to fall back on convention.

"Has orientation come to an end?" Khiri found positing questions to which she already knew the answer could be more illuminating than inquiring about the unknown.

"Yes, Abbess, just a few days ago." Chandi unconsciously rubbed a sore spot on her shoulder.

"And have you made your first supervised run?" she prodded.

"Yes, just yesterday," Chandi perked up suddenly with the direction the conversation was taking. "My group headed north as far as the Bolton's. Can you believe Willem found something on his first run?" Chandi checked herself after her impromptu familiarity with the mother of the stride; for a second, she forgot her place and present company. "Not that we run for the accumulation of wealth."

The tigress let a small smile slip. "Some sentients have all the luck."

"When I return, I begin Applied Tenets of Faith." She regained her composure and pulled a book out of her bag: *Basic Applications for the New Pathfinder.* "I thought I might get ahead." The abbess nodded her approval at the tome and permitted the pathfinder to start her reading.

The bustle of activity leading up the king's estate alerted Khiri that King Dexter VI was not only home, but entertaining guests. Their carriage waited in line while Tallis greeted each sentient as they arrived and marshaled the team of royal servants to take their baggage inside and their vehicles and steeds to the stables. She made note of their faces and regalia while the Order of the Guard held themselves steady in the presence of unknown individuals.

When the frazzled steward finally greeted the inhabitants of the church's carriage, he hardly had the energy to feign enthusiasm. "Welcome, mother and sister of the stride. The king welcomes you to his home," he began as always.

"We accept the king's hospitality and offer our humble service in tribute," Khiri replied with semi-bow and a formal nod. The abbess understood how important ritual was in the face of disruption.

The familiarity of the exchange calmed Tallis a measure. "As you can see, his highness is hosting other guests this evening, but rest assured, your customary rooms have been readied. Dinner will be in the great hall this evening, if you would like to change—"

Khiri rose to her full height before nodding curtly. "I am the mother of the stride—this is all the drapery I require." The abbess motioned for Chandi and their guards to follow, and the entourage strode into the foyer.

The great hall was a large room built of gray stone blocks that lent a frigid quality to the space that no amount of decor and wood could completely erase. The walls were decorated in a hodgepodge of tapestries, paintings, and mounted animal heads with the king's family crest hanging over an oversized fireplace. Raised candlelit chandeliers illuminated the room while others stood on the table at regular intervals.

The large oak table seated up to twenty, but according

to the settings, there were only six to dine tonight. Chandi sat beside her abbess, doing her best to remember her table manners; while the Church of Parkour was very formal in some regards, it hardly concerned itself with which utensil to use at what time. She looked around the table at her dining companions. His Royal Highness, King Dexter VI sat at the head of the table, his ornately carved seat taller than the others. A stout man just past his prime, the king's ruddy complexion was made rosy by the claret he'd imbibed. He held a goblet in one hand and a leg of meat in the other, and he ate like he spoke: loudly and with gusto. He was the first to laugh at his own jokes, which he made often, but there was a steeliness behind his mirthful eyes that always put Chandi on alert. *There is no stillness in violence.*

On either side of him sat the two Oswald brothers, their bobcat-descent heralded by their gray fur with black spots, tufts of black hair from their pointed ears, and short tails. Their undeniable likeness was made less so by their differing demeanor. Verplanck Oswald, Head Ranger of the Rangers of the Adirondack, was the elder brother, bred to his station. He wore formal attire and spoke the language of courtly influence, although none that rode with him doubted his intuition or skill in the hills. On the other hand, his younger brother, Vogler, was dressed simply in an earth-toned tabard; even that he found was too encumbering against his silvery coat. He spoke little during dinner, barely suppressing his ire over the stuffed heads hanging on the wall. Every once in a while, he would look to Khiri to gauge her reaction to such wanton displays of murdered non-mutated animals, but the tigress's face remained neutral. As Head Ranger of the Catskill Rangers, Vogler had gouged out a space for like-minded sentients that desired to be forever wild through contest with both the Lordship of the Fingers and the Hudson-Mohawk Demarchy. Vogler even pushed south into the deathlands; what place could be wilder?

Beside Vogler sat Amelia, dowager of the mountains and mother to both head rangers. Judging by the awkward glances and unspoken words between the brothers, Khiri guessed that this family reunion was the dowager's doing.

Chandi cut into her roast beast, spearing a piece of roasted potato and sprouts. While the food was much better when they dined in the great hall, she couldn't say that the atmosphere was more inviting. Although the conversation was banal and light superficially, an underlying tension quivered just beneath the surface, and even though the day was warm enough, the room seemed cold despite the blaze in the fireplace. It was shortly after dessert was served that Chandi concluded she would rather take a steak and kidney pie in the kitchen with Chef Pasleur over roast beast with the king in the great hall, all things considered. That said, the creamy filling of the flaky iced éclair was absolutely delicious.

After dinner, Dexter invited the Oswald brothers for an after-dinner drink in his study while the mother of the stride took company with the mother of the rangers, but not before advising her ward to consider taking her reading to her room tonight instead of staying late in the library. Chandi gladly made her escape and carried an armload of books to bed.

Chandi woke the next morning to the open tome she was last reading before dozing off. She perused the spines of the short stack beside her bed and picked the lightest to accompany her on her walk through the estate. She stopped by the kitchen for a quick breakfast and a cold sandwich with last night's roast beast for lunch. Chef Pasleur barked orders to her staff in preparation for lunch—there was no end to work in the kitchen: you were either preparing for a meal, serving a meal, or cleaning up after a meal—still, she found time enough to pack Chandi lunch.

The pathfinder was surprised when she ran into a member of the Order of the Guard on her way out the door. Apparently, the abbess thought it best for Chandi to have an escort during her tribute perambulation. Chandi remembered the cold stares of the Oswald brothers and decided a little company wouldn't hurt. Word must have gotten to the chef before Chandi, as she found more than enough food and drink in the basket for both herself and her guard.

Chandi was reading in the late afternoon sun at her last stop, steadying herself for another dinner in the great hall, when she heard the clamor of horses and weapons beat a hasty retreat down the long road leading away from the estate. The pathfinder made her way to house, and safely escorted back, the guard waited outside. She came in through the kitchen—whatever was happening, the servants always seemed to know—and found the abbess and chef talking quietly. Their conversation broke when they saw the pathfinder enter.

Chandi placed the now-empty basket on the counter, nodding thanks to the chef for a most pleasant lunch. "I heard horses leaving in a hurry—is something wrong?"

The two women exchanged glances and the mother of the stride spoke first, "Some business has called the king and his guests away. I'm afraid you won't have the pleasure of their company tonight at dinner." There was no trace of sarcasm in her voice or visage, merely her words.

"But you will have their dinner!" Claudette huffed; she had already had her staff working for hours toward formal dining for six.

"Would it be all right if we ate it in the kitchen?" Chandi asked cautiously.

"I think that can be arranged." The chef winked.

*****

Can you see it? I swear it's narrowing, the first spirit spoke.

It's just wishful thinking, the second dismissed.

It's not! It's not! Look—the other side is closer than it's ever been.

And yet still so far away, the second noted. It had been so long since it was home, it hadn't dared to hope again.

No one's making you keep watch, the first pointed out, but the second spirit kept his seat in front of the veil. The other side inched closer. They didn't want to call attention to themselves, but their building excitement was too much to contain.

*****

It started off small, barely heard over the din of fellowship during dinner, but as the night went on and the monastery moved to bed, everyone could hear it. Footsteps. Sometimes they were heavy and deliberate, other times clipped and fast paced. Ariadne took to the halls to investigate. As prioress, the monastery was her responsibility in Khiri's absence, and she took her duties seriously.

She reasoned that they must be intentional—even the youngest of tenderfoots could manage to walk the halls without making such a racket. Perhaps it was a prank? While it was possible, Ariadne found it hard to believe. For years she'd tended the monastery and took charge in Khiri's absence and never heard a peep or complaint from either residents or guests.

The steps were getting louder as she neared a junction. She turned the corner expecting to catch the culprit, only to find nothing. "Who's there?" she barked. "Show yourself immediately!" A high-pitched giggle erupted in the still emptiness. The steps began again, only down a different hallway. Ariadne pursued.

Her eight eyes gave her a wide field of vision, but the dim ever-lit candle she carried only cast so much light. She followed the sounds of footfalls down another passage, this one lined with glass-paned windows. She edged forward silently, the hairs on her front pair of limbs standing on edge, but picked up no vibrations in the air. She walked as far as the first window, her mirror image holding the candle moving with her. It was only after she passed it that she saw with her posterior-facing eyes the reflection of someone following her in the window: a little girl in a white dress, her hair braided in pigtails. Ariadne quickly turned around but again, no one was there. It was then the prioress turned to face the window and stared squarely at the hollow-eyed girl.

Ariadne fled away from the hall to one with no windows or mirrors, pathing her way to the door of Unseen Waters' resident sorcerer, pounding insistently with as many hands as she could muster.

"All right, all right, I'm coming!" Jackson yelled at the pounding on his door. It was never good news when someone woke the sorcerer in the middle of the night. He quickly checked his nightclothes, making sure he was decent enough before opening the door to a distressed prioress. Between the multiple pairs of limbs waving around and the numerous eyes checking to and fro, he surmised that Ariadne was having a bad night. "Give me a second to get dressed and I'll be right out."

"I'm not staying out here alone," the prioress emphatically asserted.

Jackson opened his door wide. "Then I guess you'd better come in."

Ariadne's narrative spilled forth in a jumble while the sorcerer slipped on his robes. Jackson fastened his sheathed dagger on his hip and shined his belt buckle.

"Slow down; let's start from the beginning," he counseled her, pushing a small tumbler of watered-down whisky her way. "It started out as steps?" Ariadne took a sip and grimaced, but it didn't stop her from taking another before replying.

"That's how it started," the shaken prioress answered.

"And they giggled at you?"

"Yes, like it was playing or laughing at me. And just when I thought I'd caught up with it, it would move again." She fidgeted in her chair. Jackson leaned back, giving her some space.

"So how does the mirror-girl come into this?"

"I followed the steps to the far western hallway, where the glass windows are. That's where I saw her following me."

"But not actually following you, just in the reflection," Jackson clarified.

"Yes, a pretty little thing in a white dress and hair in braids…" she answered, her voice fading to a whisper. "But she had no eyes, just emptiness where they should be."

Jackson rubbed the stubble on the chin and grabbed a few things from his shelves. "Stay here. I'll be back in a bit." Ariadne was not one to take orders from anyone but the abbess, but on this occasion, she kept her seat and watched Jackson close the door behind him.

The sorcerer focused on the chatter as he walked the empty halls of the monastery. There seemed to be more activity than usual—the otherworld was excited about something. He headed for the far western hallway, the last place the prioress experienced contact. "Step fear," someone whispered in his ear. "Spirit of mischief."

Jackson drew his dagger with one hand and reached into a pouch with another, sprinkling a little sugar in a circle, murmuring words in his sorcerous tongue. The air grew cold around him and the sounds of steps and laughter tripped over each other as they swelled to a crescendo. None could break the silence Jackson found within, and inside the sugary circle appeared the hollow-eyed little girl described by the prioress. Jackson raised his blade and spoke to her in their shared secret language, "It's time to go to bed." He stabbed her heart and the girl's body collapsed into the wound, like the beginning of a black hole. Once her form was nothing more than a speck of emptiness, Jackson nudged it into his buckle with the end of his dagger.

The rest of the evening passed without incident and all was quiet in the Monastery of Unseen Waters, but the resident sorcerer found no stillness in the night. He couldn't calm down that niggling notion that something was wrong. A spirit of discord in the ruins *and* a spirit of mischief in the monastery within days of each other? He was never one to put much stock in happenstance—his mother use to say, "Once is an accident, twice is a coincidence, three times is a pattern."

After Ariadne finished morning devotion, Jackson hung around the hall and reinforced the wards of the four cardinal pillars—something he should do more regularly, but it hardly seemed necessary given the usual lack of spirit activity in the monastery. Usually. Should something bigger break through the veil, at least this space was safe and all the inhabitants of the monastery fit inside, as evidenced by morning devotion.

His suspicion proved warranted when a coddle-woddle appeared in the courtyard during afternoon meditation as a three-foot-tall teddy bear. Generally it was thought of as a protector spirit, inducing crying children to calm and sleep in its ghostly otherworld form. The problem arose when it was made flesh under the shattered moon; the coddle-woddle didn't know when to stop its affection, slowly squeezing the air and life out of the child that it so wanted to be its friend. Jackson quickly dispatched the stuff-and-fluff from the courtyard and advised the instructors to move the students into the main hall within the wards while he checked the grounds.

Jackson cleared the courtyard and walked the perimeter, gardens, workshops, and barns. He roamed the passageways of the monastery, letting the voices of the otherworld wash over him. It wasn't something he did often, but he didn't have a lead. Someone must know something; the problem with this method was discerning the wheat from the chaff, but at least he had something to work with. He found no other spirits on his perambulation, but the same word kept arising throughout the monastery: moonstone.

Both Ariadne and Jackson were waiting for the carriage when Khiri and Chandi returned from their tribute trip. Khiri quickly went inside while Chandi headed to her room, both eager to find out what precipitated a welcoming party.

*****

"Wait, a real live spirit? Made flesh?!" Chandi exclaimed.

"Yes! It just popped up in the middle of the courtyard between the mats and the walls," Lucy confirmed. "It sort of looked cute, but in a creepy way."

Chandi shivered; she had never been a teddy bear sort of girl. "I can't believe I missed it! I've been here eleven years and the first time there is an actual being from the otherworld, I'm not here."

"Everyone was freaking out and the instructors were trying to keep everyone away from it, but it kept waddling around and saying things like 'Don't you want to hold me?' and 'Can you come out and play?' And then Jackson comes out of nowhere, tells everyone to get the main hall, and pulls out this giant dagger!"

"No way!"

"I know, right! He starts chanting in some weird language and starts wailing on it; stuffing flies everywhere but magically disappears into his belt buckle."

"His belt buckle?" she incredulously challenged her roommate's account.

"His belt buckle." Lucy stated adamantly.

Chandi lay back in her bed and sighed. "The otherworld is so messed up."

"Yup."

*****

"You're sure you heard that right—moonstone?" Khiri quizzed the sorcerer.

"Yes, Abbess. Does that mean anything to you?" Jackson had tried to elicit more information from the spirits but he came up blank.

"No, but we have to think about the safety of the monastery." Khiri turned to the prioress. "Notify Aren that we will have an increased Order of the Guard presence within the monastery walls. Training and meditation will continue, but pathfinders and tracers in the ruins must be on high alert and never run alone." Khiri paused for the prioress to take note. The abbess knew everyone was supposed to only run the ruins in septs, but she also knew the temperament of runners. "Any finds in the ruins must be cleared by Jackson before entering the walls. We will take additional precautions with all visitors: conduct interviews and searches for any possible items that may have triggered the uptick in spirit activity."

"I've already reinforced the wards in the main hall and cleared the area within the walls right before your return," Jackson reported. "Is there anything you need me to do, Abbess?"

Khiri gave him a stern look. "Keep your blade sharp."

*****

He was gone. It didn't think it would miss him, but now that he had crossed to the other side, the vigil of the veil seemed emptier and less vital. It was his time—he saw the children at play, running and jumping. How long had it been since children played on the moon? For that matter, how long had it been since it fractured? How could he resist the call when the chasm had narrowed enough for him to leap across?

It didn't fault him for leaving, but it wasn't happy about it, either. And now the chasm expands again, waxing and waning as the moon does in the Earth's sky. While it was only left with longing and sadness, the rest of the voices in Moonstone focused on the facts: someone had crossed the chasm.

Chapter Eleven

The abbess took to the dais for morning devotion—it waited for no one, not even the otherworld. A nervous energy buzzed throughout the hall, but Khiri had faith she could lead them to stillness in time. An announcement afterward informed the monastery at large of the precautionary measures that would be taken in the upcoming days. Otherwise, life proceeded as usual, albeit with the Order of the Guard and a pacing sorcerer in their midst. The spirit chatter was back to its normal hum and the frenetic voices of yesterday were gone, making Jackson feel like the entire otherworld was ghosting him—no pun intended.

All the pupils were relieved to hear that meditation would continue, especially the pathfinders who were due to run the ruins that day. The visitors each took their turn with Ariadne and Jackson while Khiri regained command of the monastery.

For the pathfinder trainees, today was the first session of Applied Tenets of Faith, and they were uncertain what to expect. It was taught by meditation instructors, not scholars, and the classroom was littered with stations of mats. The book

Chandi brought during her tribute visit was of little help—it was mostly diagrams of posed figures with arrows pointing in various directions. It looked suspiciously like a manual for fighting hand-to-hand, but the author's preface assured the gentle reader that this was *not* combat, merely another means to flow like water over the land should they encounter an opponent from which they could not hide, evade, or simply outrun.

Dendra started the didactic portion and the principles sounded familiar enough: *stillness of mind can overcome a body in action, an opponent's aggression is used against them by evading and redirecting,* and *aim for efficiency in engagements—use minimum effort for maximum effect.* She called Netu and Tracer Lee to the front for a demonstration. Mika lunged toward the scritcher, who deftly grabbed Mika's arms, twisted down and sideways, and flipped the tracer to the mat. The pathfinders were speechless.

"Now clearly, you won't start there," Dendra tried to temper their awe. "But with practice and training, it is possible." She dismissed Netu and Mika from the front. "We are going to pair up and start with basic forms. It does not matter who you pair up with now; over the course of training, you will practice with all pathfinders. Proceed."

Predictably Mira and Natalie moved to a mat while the others made quick pairings—no one wanted to be pricked by Jukka's thorns all afternoon. Chandi's search for a partner stalled as Mika and Netu passed by.

"Next time, I get to be the one doing the throwing," Mika ribbed Netu.

Netu laughed. "Seeing as you're leaving tomorrow, I'll take my chances." Sensing the feel of the room, Dendra offered to partner with Jukka as she was immune to his natural herbaceous defenses, but that left Chandi without a partner.

"Looks like you are the odd man out." Mika approached her from the side. "I'll be your partner today." Chandi let out a sigh of relief. "But tomorrow, you'll have to partner faster than that to avoid the thorns," Mika spoke in a low soft tone.

"So you're leaving tomorrow?" she asked politely while adopting the lunging form Bibi and Lars modeled in front.

"Yeah, I was supposed to leave yesterday afternoon, but with the commotion, my transport was delayed until tomorrow morning." Mika matched the bend of her knees, his right leg in back. He held out his left hand and Chandi placed her palm against his.

"I'm glad—not for the giant teddy bear terrorizing the courtyard—but that you got to stay another day. Otherwise, I wouldn't have been able to wish you good pathing to your next assignment." They pushed against each other, testing their relative strength. A clap from the front of the room broke the tension, indicating it was time to change to the other side. Chandi repositioned and held out her right hand this time.

*****

Chandi hid among the rows in the garden, peering up at the bright full moon. A few clouds dotted the sky, but otherwise it was just her and moon in contemplation. The abbess kept precautions in place despite Jackson's all clear, but Chandi found sneaking past warriors of the Order of the Guard cake compared to an actual church member—you could hear the guards coming from a mile away, and they didn't train to see the unseen like runners do.

Occasionally she heard passing patrols but mostly she was left with her thoughts. She had been driven to distraction ever since she found out Mika was leaving in the morning. She had gotten used to his presence and the news of his leaving caused her no end of consternation. She had hoped to have more time—to talk to him, get to know him better, have him know her better—but that wasn't going to happen. Like Chandi, tracers went where they were needed.

She couldn't figure out what was stopping her. She knew which room was his, and as long as a spirit didn't become flesh in that very room, no one in the monastery was going to care. The church took a practical view on sex: as long as it was consensual and didn't disrupt the functioning of the monastery, they didn't care what a sentient did from dinner till morning devotion, as long as they fit in evening reflection somewhere in there. And the sorcerous sigil all the runners brandished ensured it wouldn't interfere with their meditation.

There wasn't anything wrong with Mika. He was kind. And funny. He didn't take himself too seriously, and to quote Lucy, "That ass!" And when he looked at her with those violet eyes, she felt both still and running at the same time. So what was it?

She had messed around with other sentients before, mostly to see what all the fuss was about, but she never felt interested in going all the way. At least not until recently. Somebody had to be the first, and she was kind of hoping it would be Mika. Maybe that was the problem—she actually wanted Mika. What if he said "no"?

The part of Lucy she carried with her emphatically stated he would be a moron to say "no." The analytical part of her brain reasoned that made tonight all the more perfect time. If he said "no," he would be gone in the morning. If he said "yes" and it went terrible, he would be gone in the morning. If he said "yes" and it was great, at least she had that time with him before he would be gone in the morning. Rationally, it made sense, but some decisions had little to do with reason. In the stillness of the calm night, her heart told her she would regret not trying. She looked up at the moon and sighed. She already knew what she was going to do; now she just had to muster the courage.

It was late when Chandi re-entered the monastery and crept to the visitors' section. She stared at his door, going over what she was going to say, how she was going to be. Finally, she knocked softly, hoping it was loud enough to for him to hear because she was not prepared to knock a second time. There were noises from the other side before the handle finally turned.

Mika was in his nightclothes, his short hair slightly disheveled, and a little groggy with sleep but awake. Chandi froze and couldn't speak; all her prepared, nonchalant words left her head. So she did what she did best—she moved and let her arms guide her motion. She placed a hand on either side of his face, stepped up on her toes, and kissed him. His mouth was warm and she could taste the mint on his breath from the tea served at dinner. She could feel how close he was without actually touching the rest of his body, and she deepened the kiss.

It took her a second to realize he wasn't kissing her back. *Why isn't he kissing me back?* His hand was still on the door handle and the other one hung limply at his side. Chandi panicked and broke contact abruptly. "My apologies, Brother Mika. I merely wanted to wish you good pathing tomorrow, but I see I have interrupted your slumber. May stillness find you in the night." She turned around with every intent of finding the quickest path to her bed to die of embarrassment when she felt a hand on her arm.

"Chandi, wait," Mika broke his silence. Chandi paused her retreat as Mika shook the sleep from his head. "I wasn't expecting you. You just caught me off guard…" Chandi winced. "But it was nice." Mika immediately regretted his word choice while Chandi considered how she felt about "nice."

Mika released his hold and leaned against the door. "What I meant to say is, now that I'm up, would you like to come inside and try for better than nice?"

Chandi noted the change in his voice and turned to face him. "I don't know…I thought tracers were supposed to be the elite of the elite. Can't be that good when you're surprised by a pathfinder-in-training."

Mika laughed and his violet eyes danced. "To be fair, I don't often run in my sleep or in my nightclothes. But you should probably come in, for my own safety."

Chandi passed just inside the threshold of his door and Mika took a step toward her, closing both the door and the space between them.

*****

Chandi opened the door to her room and quietly slinked in. It wasn't until the door was closed behind her that Lucy spoke. "And where have you been?!"

"Shh! You want to wake the whole monastery?"

Lucy whispered her question this time. "So where were you? I was worried. You could have been spirit food by now."

"Do spirits-made-flesh even need to eat?" Chandi wondered

"Don't change the subject."

"I was looking at the moon—" Chandi answered, changing into her nightclothes.

"For three hours?" Lucy asked skeptically.

"You didn't let me finish. I was looking at the moon before stopping by Mika's room to wish him good pathing to his new assignment tomorrow."

Lucy froze in her top bunk. "Hunky Mika, with the nice ass and the blue eyes?"

"His eyes are violet," Chandi corrected her roommate. Lucy could hardly contain her squeal.

"So," Lucy started delicately, "what happened?"

"We talked a little and did other stuff," Chandi answered vaguely.

"So like kissing other stuff, or beast with two backs other stuff?"

"That's a wide field of variance, Lucy," Chandi chided. "Why don't you just ask me what you want to know."

"If you know what I want to ask, why don't you just tell me," Lucy baited.

Chandi smiled at her obtuse best friend. "Mission accomplished on Operation Cherry Bomb."

Lucy popped her head down from the top bunk. "Are you freaking kidding me?!"

"Done and dusted," Chandi confirmed.

"Did it hurt?"

"Like hell at first, but it got better," Chandi fondly recalled

Mika's warm mouth on her breast as he slowly eased his way in.

Lucy's tone softened. "How do you feel?"

Chandi didn't know how to answer. "Okay, I guess. I mean, it was fine…better than fine. It was fun and he was sweet. But I'm still me. Clearly, things are different and I'm different. I don't know, I just thought I would be *more* different…"

Lucy pulled her head up and let the silence sit for a while before talking. "If you could go back in time, would you still do it?"

Chandi didn't need to think long before answering, "Yes."

"That's what's important. The rest you'll sort it out in time." Lucy stretched and yawned. "Your first time is always weird—it takes time to put everything in its place and make sense of it." Lucy froze and was suddenly wide awake; she'd picked up on her slip a second too late.

"Lucy, are you trying to tell me something…"

Lucy lay very still in her top bunk. "Six months ago."

"And you didn't tell me?!"

"Now who's going to wake the entire monastery?" Lucy whispered.

Chandi composed herself. "Not that you had to tell me, but why didn't you?"

"You were never into that sort of thing. If it wasn't a book or running, you weren't interested. Plus, I didn't want you to think differently about me."

"Lucy, you could sleep with the entire monastery three

times over and I couldn't care less, although I would wonder where you found the time…"

Lucy giggled.

"Am I allowed to ask who?"

"Only if you promise not to laugh."

Chandi chose her next words carefully. "I promise to try really hard not to laugh, but now you have to tell me."

Lucy crinkled her nose. "Willem."

"I'm sorry, did you say 'Willem'?"

"You promised not to laugh!"

"I'm *not* laughing," Chandi stated firmly. "How exactly did that happen?"

"He was super bummed about failing the pathfinder trials again and I was trying to point out all his good qualities to lift his mood. One thing led to another and…yeah."

"So was this a one-off or a regular thing?" Chandi asked out of morbid curiosity. *Willem*?!

"Well, we aren't planning on quitting running and having babies anytime soon, but I can't honestly say it was a one-off. He was really great after pathfinder trials, and I know he can come off as brusque at times, but he can be really sensitive when he wants to be."

"Just promise me you guys don't do it in my bed while I'm away for the tribute visit."

"It is two nights every month…" Lucy needled.

"Lucy!"

"What, don't act like he hasn't tried his luck with you."

"Willem?! No."

Lucy's head dropped into Chandi's view again. "While you were helping him train, did he ever sit a little too close, give you a goofy grin, and nudge your arm with his?"

"Yeah, but that's just Willem—wait, are you telling me that's his move?"

Lucy flipped her head back to her pillow. "I'm not saying it's the smoothest one, but he does take full ownership of it."

Chandi thought back to all those times she just thought Willem was being a goofball. "So how many other times have sentients been hitting on me and I was clueless."

Lucy laughed. "I lost count a long time ago. Credit where it's due—you've pretty much brushed everyone off uniformly."

"When Charlie offered to swap evening chores in the barn?"

"Yup."

"When Dodger let me use the slack line before him even though he was waiting first?

"Yup."

"And when Lena offered to spot me on the wall?"

"Yeah, and she is still offering to help me with my Kong vault. If that is not a euphemism, I don't know what is."

"So I should just assume that everyone that offers to do something nice for me is trying to get in my pants?" Chandi groaned.

"No, but thinking that it's never the reason is going too far in the other direction." Lucy tried to think of an appropriate explanation. "It's not so much they all want to sleep with you, but think of it as an opening salvo. If they are nice to you and you are nice to them, maybe you could be nice to each other together." Given the silence from the lower bunk, Lucy kept digging. "You are wonderful all the way around, and it's probably not a bad assumption for you to consider that sentients might want to get close to you when they interact with you. You aren't obligated to say 'yes' to all of them, just the ones you want to get close to as well."

Chandi could live with that, and a soft "huh" from below let Lucy know she had gotten through. The quiet settled in the room, but Lucy could feel the unrest.

"Do you want me to come down?"

"No, it's all right," Chandi took a little too long to answer. "It's late and morning devotion waits for no one."

Lucy grabbed her pillow and blanket and landed softly on the floor. Chandi moved over to make room. Lucy wedged herself behind Chandi and put an arm over her waist. "No dreams about running," Lucy asserted. "We aren't as little as we use to be and the beds certainly haven't gotten bigger."

Cradled against her best friend in the full moon's light, Chandi found the stillness in the night between Lucy's deep breaths.

Chapter Twelve

Jackson didn't know which irritated him more, that he couldn't find anything out about "moonstone" or that all the spirit activity had completely died down. He and Ariadne conducted all the interviews and searched all the visitors and ruin finds for something sorcerous in nature, but everything came up dry. After a week, the abbess called off the extra precautions and the Order of the Guard resumed normal activity, but Jackson continued to reinforce the wards in the main hall, just in case.

When he drew a blank, he consulted the scholars, again, a move he rarely made. Much of their "scholarship" was doctrine related, so he went to the only resident scholar with a scientific bone in his body: Brother Bartholomew. That old bird had seen and heard of everything, so when he drew a blank on moonstone, Jackson didn't have much hope. Still, Bartholomew promised to dig into his library and the sorcerer had high hopes when Bartholomew asked him to stop by his quarters after dinner.

Jackson brought his bottle of whiskey to wet the owl's whistle and placed three short raps on his door. Through the thick wood, he could hear him rise to open the door—Jackson figured he must have found something if he was answering his door instead of yelling his customary "Enter." The owl motioned him in to the set of chairs and waved his other hand toward some glasses for the amber liquid in Jackson's hand. Jackson started pouring while Bartholomew hovered over a few open books at his desk.

"I see you have been busy." The sorcerer raised his drink to his host before taking a swig.

"I've always loved a good puzzle," Bartholomew replied before tasting the contents of his glass. It wasn't bad, but it wasn't brandy; he set the glass down. "I found references to moonstones, which are a precious gem of the ancients, but not actually from the lunar body." He placed an open book in front of Jackson. "It's actually a feldspar, only the cleaving and refraction of light gives it a pearly or opalescent sheen. It was thought to have healing powers and had strong associations with the moon and feminine energies, but I have yet to find any contemporary sources that support such claims."

"Then there is moon rock, which is actually from the lunar body but not nearly as pretty." The scholar pulled another tome out and laid it in front of the sorcerer. "Apparently, the ancients also had a fascination with them; they brought some back to Earth when they first landed on the moon. Your people really are totemic."

Jackson chuckled privately at Bartholomew's assertion,

first that Jackson had anything in common with the ancients just because he was human; and second, that the owl was disparaging faith beliefs and totems when he was a scholar of a church that literally believes everyone under the shattered moon is stuck here because in some past life, they didn't run away fast enough from the apocalypse. Still, the sorcerer didn't argue and simply took another sip.

There was another knock on his door. Bartholomew yelled "Enter!" out of habit before taking a seat and lighting his pipe. "I'm afraid none of my texts can tie either moon rocks or moonstones to increased spirit activity under the shattered moon," he addressed Jackson before looking to the door. "Chandi, are you all right? You look as white as a sheet!"

"Did you say 'Moonstone'?" she uttered, and Jackson ushered her to a seat before her knees buckled. As a sorcerer, he'd had his fair share of talking sentients down when they were in shock, and his intuition was that this kid knew something about moonstone.

He generously watered down Bartholomew's glass and gave it to Chandi. "Here, take a sip, catch your breath, and start from the beginning." The pathfinder obeyed and her face winced at the sharpness of the whiskey, but it did bring the color back to her face.

"It's a meteorite I found in the monastery grounds. It fell from the sky one night and I picked it up. It glowed in the moonlight—I thought it was a sign about the upcoming pathfinder trials." She looked up at Brother Bartholomew then turned toward the sorcerer. "Do you really think it's responsible for the spirits?"

"How long ago was this?" Jackson redirected her focus.

"A little less than two months ago."

"When you found it, did it talk to you? Tell you its name was Moonstone?"

"No, it's a rock and rocks don't talk." Chandi looked at him oddly. "I gave it the name Moonstone because it fell from the sky during a full moon," she explained.

"Do you have it now?" Jackson spoke in an even tone. You get use to sentients thinking you are crazy when you hear voices in your head all the time.

"Not on me, but it's in my room."

"Does anyone else know about it?"

Chandi shook her head.

"Not even Miss Montenegro?" Bartholomew interjected.

"No," Chandi confirmed.

"Good. I want you to go back to your room, fetch it, and bring it back here," Jackson instructed her. Chandi nodded. "And not a word to anyone until we figure out what it is and if it's important." The pathfinder left the scholar's room in a daze.

*****

Khiri turned the rock around in her hands. "It's such an

111

unassuming thing," she commented.

"It's not much to look at," Jackson agreed. "I've done some rudimentary tests on it, and there doesn't seem to be anything otherworldly about it."

Khiri put it down on her desk. "Perhaps it's just a coincidence? It may have nothing to do at all with the spirit activity."

Jackson shifted uneasily. "I don't like coincidences."

"No, neither do I," the abbess confessed, and bit her lower lip. "Has Bartholomew had a chance to run any tests?"

"Not yet. I just got my hands on it a few days ago, and I've done every test I can think of."

"And she said it glowed in the light of the moon?"

"Apparently that what drew her to keep it, as a good luck charm," Jackson relayed. "But hell if I can get it to glow."

Khiri sighed. "Tell me honestly, have you ever heard of such a thing—a rock that draws out spirit activity? Because I haven't."

"There are spirits that live in rocks—elementals or fairies— but I can't find any evidence of such in this piece," Jackson qualified.

The tigress rose to her feet and started pacing while she thought. Her pinpoint pupils and the swish of her tail set Jackson's primitive hindbrain on edge. "Let Bartholomew conduct his tests and if everything comes back clear, we have done our due diligence," she decreed.

Jackson pocketed the stone and gave a semi-formal bow. "Yes, Abbess."

*****

The warm air of summer blew through the carriage carrying Khiri and Chandi as the horses came to full speed. The early portion had passed in silence, and the pathfinder wasn't sure where to look in the cabin, so she pulled out a book instead. Chandi knew the abbess knew about Moonstone, and Khiri knew that Chandi knew, but not a word about it was spoken between them. Khiri was accustomed to the right hand not knowing what the left hand held, but the pathfinder felt strange sharing a secret with the abbess. It made the tigress seem simultaneously more mysterious and more relatable, not that Chandi and she would be having late night heart-to-hearts anytime soon.

"What book have you today, sister of the stride?"

"The same as last time, Abbess; I wasn't able to get a new book before leaving. If I'm being honest, I didn't really understand what the illustrations meant the first time I read it, but Applied Tenets of Faith has helped me unlock the book's meaning," Chandi replied diplomatically. Chandi had been so startled by hearing Brothers Bartholomew and Jackson discuss Moonstone, she had forgotten to exchange books.

"I have no doubt you will quickly grasp the basics," the

abbess replied neutrally. "If memory serves me right, you already mastered the leg sweep many years ago."

Chandi looked up from her book and found the tigress looking out the window, no sign of emotion in her face but a slight flick of the end of her tail.

*****

Jackson took his coffee amidst a flurry of activity in the kitchen. It started when the cook couldn't find her ladle. It was the perfect ladle for breakfast, because the porridge didn't stick to it like it did with the others. She insisted that the ladle always hung on that hook and it was there when she put the kitchen to bed last night, but when she came down this morning, it was gone.

In his years, the sorcerer had seen it before—sentients were quick to blame the spirits for everything, especially after a recent scare. The mind wanted to find reason to settle a restless heart. Not that they couldn't cause mischief—there were plenty of preservative and elemental spirits with a penchant of impishness— but if the worst they did was move your ladle, they probably weren't the malevolent sort that required Jackson's skills and could be otherwise appeased. "Put out a dish of sugar or honey in a bit of milk tonight, and I'm sure your ladle will turn up," the sorcerer recommended knowingly.

He returned to his room to gear up for another patrol of

114

the ruins. The sorcerer methodically checked and donned his equipment before meeting the Order of the Guard outside the gates. Like the monastery, the ruins had quieted down in the weeks after Jackson dispatched the altered state, but vigilance bore its own fruit. Plus, it was a nice day, far too warm and sunny to be in one's room crafting spells.

He lunched with the guards— there was only so much pottage a man could eat—and returned to the monastery in good cheer. There was a commotion in the courtyard amongst the novices when he returned.

"He loosened the winch while I was on the line!" one sentient accused another.

"I didn't! It looked loose, and I was coming over to tighten it," the other sentient defended himself.

An instructor examined the machinery. "It's working fine now. Everyone back to your meditation!"

Times like this made Jackson glad he was human. As a sorcerer, his contribution to the church was in services, not in instruction. While the children of the monastery were some of the most disciplined under the shattered moon, they were still kids. Sure, someone had to teach the next generation, but it didn't have to be him. At least not yet. He knew he was overdue to take on an apprentice, but as long as he was tucked away at the Monastery of Unseen Waters, the church wouldn't chance disclosure. It wasn't like young sorcerers were coming out of the woodwork; humans became a rare breed after the moon shattered.

Jackson was through the better half of a treatise on necromantic spirits when the prioress barged through his door. "The infirmary," was all she said before turning on her heels. He grabbed his kit and followed Ariadne.

*****

"Let me get this straight." Jackson consulted his notes. "You're saying the wall moved in the adaptive training ground."

"Yes," Yan replied simply.

"But isn't that what it's supposed to do? That's why they call it the adaptive training ground—things can be moved."

The petite pathfinder fought hard not to roll her eyes. "Not in the middle of practice. One second my foot is on target to hit the wall, the next, I'm inches away and falling flat on my side." One of the attendants was wrapping Yan's ankle and applying an unguent on her abraded skin. "I *don't* unintentionally fall when I run."

"Anyone else having problems in training today?" Jackson inquired—he was getting that niggling feeling again.

"No one injured, per se, but we were all off this morning. Except for Chandi—she wasn't at meditation today."

Jackson thanked Yan for her time and drew the prioress to the side. "Could be nothing, but I'll go to the training ground and take a look around. Are there any students in there now?"

"There shouldn't be." The prioress was always very precise with her words.

The simulation zone was still in the late afternoon heat but it was far from quiet, at least to Jackson. Something had the otherworld riled up; everyone was talking and it was up to him to figure out who to listen to. There were echoes of "moonstone" from different sources; Jackson tried to elicit more, but only got a few words—the chasm is closing—before it became gibberish to even him.

As someone who patrolled the ruins regularly, he rarely had cause to enter the training ground, but as it was still within the monastery walls, there shouldn't be anything regenerating here. Jackson regarded the faux ruins like the shadow of a real place. In some ways it was creepier in here, and that was quite a claim coming from him.

He felt a ripple of energy course through the air as he tripped on an uneven piece of plascrete. At least he thought that's what it was, but when he looked back, the ground was smooth and level. "Miscalculation," reverberated in his ears. "Spirit of disorder." Jackson was lenient with the small spirits, but he had to draw the line somewhere, and injuring pathfinders was a hard "no."

The sorcerer's incantations rang in the arena as he found the silence within and pulled out a fine white powder from a pocket. Jackson rubbed the chalk dust between his fingers as he formed a triangle in the air with his hand. His other hand made for his dagger. Out of the aerial triangle emerged a small creature wearing a pointy hat and dressed in colorful clothing, not unlike the lawn statutes that once graced yard-proud homes before the moon shattered, only this creature was gaunt. Its skin stretched too taut over bony prominences and its ill-fitting clothes hung at odd angles.

The sorcerer drew it out with his litany of words, even as it squirmed and fought to keep its ghostly form. Jackson drew his dagger and sliced the creature's belly. A myriad of light spilled out from its gut, and Jackson commanded the prism into his belt buckle. "Off by none."

Chapter Thirteen

Brother Bartholomew rolled the smooth stone in one hand. *It would take time*, he thought to himself, *but good analysis usually does*. His workshop tables were cleared and strewn with books and folios instead of their usual crucibles and test tubes for this inquiry. In the past few days, the scholar had located all references to geology and meteorites in his collection and had them arranged to suit his investigations.

Gross visual inspection quickly ruled out the feldspar gem; there were no lines of cleavage to account for even an uncut specimen to be hidden in this chunk. The owl held the rock under bright light and examined it under magnification—no hint of strata, cracks, fissures, or voids. He held a compass to it and the needle did not vary or twitch. Bartholomew considered that it could be moon rock despite the discrepancy in its appearance to the pictures in his book. After all, those samples were extracted on the moon and brought back to Earth in a spaceship or capsule; this rock fell from space and passed through the atmosphere. Such intense heat and pressure would certainly change its appearance, but that shouldn't change its composition.

According to his references, a chemical analysis was in order: the mineral content of rock from the moon was very sparse and fell within set parameters compared to rocks from Earth. As he did not have a mass spectrometer—whatever that was—he would have to rely on various solutions to glean information. After some deliberation over a pipe, he considered the best line of exploration was to test for minerals that *shouldn't* be found in a lunar rock—that would definitely prove that this specimen was *not* from the moon. If he could find no traces of those common Earth minerals in this stone, it wouldn't prove it was lunar in nature, but it would be highly suggestive.

The owl was so caught up in his plotting that he didn't hear Jackson's first knock on his door, but the second broke his reverie. "Did you find anything out, Bartholomew?" the sorcerer skipped all pleasantries.

"It's not the gem moonstone, but I'm trying to determine if it is in fact a lunar meteorite," Bartholomew answered. The scholar proceeded to delineate his line of inquiry and testing to which Jackson politely nodded until he heard the voices in the stillness that came with boredom.

"Shh," the sorcerer cut him off mid-sentence. "Do you hear that?" The murmur of voices was faint but audible.

The scholar sat in silence, baffled. "Hear what?" he finally asked.

A knot formed in Jackson's gut. "Bartholomew, step away

from the stone."

*****

The news of a spirit crossing to the other side spread through Moonstone; the curious and the skeptical alike came to watch but all they saw was the chasm as it was before, an abyss that kept them from daring to pierce the veil. The ones who had dared to hope were the angriest with the lone witness.

You liar! The chasm is as wide as ever.

I swear, he crossed; the chasm narrowed and he crossed!

How can the gaping abyss wax and wane?

Is that not what the moon appears to do from Earth?

The argument raged until a spirit piped up, breaking the debate. *Look—the other side of the veil is nearing!*

You see, I told you! The chasm is closing, a wounded voice declared defensively.

Smaller spirits skittered up and down the length of the veil. The more daring took a running jump through the veil aiming for the other side—some falling into oblivion, others just barely making it. The pensive spirit in the back watched the frenzy of activity. He knew he was too large, that there would be too much resistance for him to pass through the veil *and* make it to the other side. Nonetheless, his spectral heart beat fast—the gap was closing. Soon, the other side would be close enough. He had waited this long to come home; he could wait a little longer.

✳✳✳✳✳

"You want to do what?!" Ariadne yelped. Jackson knew she wouldn't like it, but he hadn't anticipated her pitch leaving his hearing registry.

"Hear me out, Ariadne," Jackson replied calmly.

"That's Prioress or Sister Ariadne to you," she corrected him.

Jackson sighed. "Prioress, I think it's the best way to protect the monastery, at least until the abbess returns tomorrow evening."

"The main hall is our holiest of spaces. It is a sanctuary for both stillness and fellowship. It's our refuge from spirit activity. And now you want to use it as a ghost prison?" she finished indignantly.

"I've looked at this every way I know how. Something is coming through, but it can't pass through the veil yet. All of the otherworld is talking about it. Somehow it is connected to this." Jackson held up Moonstone. "If we can neutralize it, maybe it won't come through. And if it comes through anyway, better to limit where its made-flesh form can roam."

"Those wards are for keeping spirits out; what makes you think you can turn it into a cage to keep a spirit-made-flesh in?"

"I don't know for sure," Jackson admitted, "but everything I understand about the wards implies that it is at least possible."

"Well, can't you just make a little box and put some wards on that? Wouldn't that contain it?" Ariadne conjectured.

The sorcerer shook his head. "Do you know how long those wards have been up? How many sorcerer-hours it took to create them? I'm just the maintenance guy that cleans and tops them off every once in a while. There is no way I could create something like that whole cloth in a couple of hours." Ariadne folded her arms in displeasure and a cast fell over her face. Jackson knew that look—she was hunkering down and he had little time to change her mind.

He took a deep breath, said a little prayer to whoever was listening, and hoped that history still carried a little weight. "Ariadne," he spoke her name with a quiet tenderness he hadn't for years, "if I thought there was another way, I would have offered that first, but right now it's our best hope. That giant teddy bear is nothing compared to what is coming through. So far, all the spirit activity has been in the realm of protective and elemental spirits—small nuances that are annoying but generally harmless until they are made flesh. But something bigger is coming, something necromantic, and I don't know how else to protect everyone while I take care of it when it arrives."

The prioress paused, clicking the tips of her chitinous legs on the stone floor. Jackson counted fifty before the prioress called the sub-prior into the room. "The main hall is off limits to the monastery at large and is to be locked. Access is to be limited to myself or Brother Jackson. We will be holding morning devotion in the courtyard for the next few days. Ready the area and notify Aren that a squad of the Order of the Guard will be stationed outside of the main hall until the abbess returns." After the sub-prior left, Ariadne focused all eight of her eyes on Jackson. "You better be right about this."

Jackson smiled. "If I'm wrong, you can blame it all on me." *Like she needed my permission....* He hurried to the main hall to start work immediately, touching every ward and speaking in his sorcerous tongue. It was the best he could do tonight. He tucked the stone in a small sack and placed it in the middle of the hall, equidistant to each of the wards.

"Are you sure this will work?" Bartholomew called from the entrance, puffing away on a pipe.

"Do you really want me to answer that truthfully?" Jackson called back. The old bird must really be intrigued if he resisted the call of his armchair for his evening smoke.

Bartholomew guffawed. "When you get older, you understanding just how much you don't know. It makes the world a scarier place—even though reality has not changed, merely your perception of it."

"Careful, Bartholomew, you are walking a fine line toward Pensivism," Jackson teased as he closed and locked the doors behind him.

*****

Why has it slowed? a strapping voice demanded.

Has it? a meek cry squeaked. *The chasm still looks to be closing to me,* it said reassuringly.

But the other side moves closer at a snail's pace!

You have waited this long; what's a little longer?

*****

Sunrise came without event and the Monastery of Unseen Waters sat as one in stillness as it had always done. The incense filled the dewy morning air and the turn of the prayer wheel joined the bird song. The Order of the Guard kept their position just outside of the closed main hall as a precaution. The prioress was both relieved and annoyed they were unneeded—there was no way to definitively prove you'd avoided a negative without removing precautions and having catastrophe follow.

With disaster averted for one night, Jackson turned his attention to the stone. The voices he heard from it didn't dwell in the stone like nature elementals did. It was almost like the voices were talking *through* it. He couldn't communicate to the beings on the other side of the veil like he normally could, so he settled for the next best thing. He asked the spirits of deceased sorcerers in the otherworld for their insight; knowledge that came at a price, but he had run out of lines of inquiry. He knew it was a necromantic spirit and it was big, but that was all he knew.

Jackson released a small piece of himself as he muttered his sorcerous tongue. A flutter of replies answered, all vying for the morsel of the living sorcerer's essence. Jackson settled on one who seemed to have more to offer. *Spirit of despair and longing,* breathed into his ear, *countered with pearl of hope.* This was the downside of dealing with dead sorcerers—they were always trying to upsell the spells they'd crafted during their life. It was the sorcerer's path to immortality—get enough people to use your spells, collect enough living essence, and get reborn again. Jackson didn't hold it against any ghostly sorcerer in particular, rather against the entire scheme. Still, it had to be better than death, didn't it?

Armed with more knowledge about what might be coming through, the sorcerer switched his focus to a different facet of this strange affair: the pathfinder who'd turned in Moonstone. While Jackson generally kept out of the educational aspects of the monastery, he knew where the student archives were. For an institution so focused on movement, the Church of Parkour kept impeccable records.

Chandini Choudary joined the church eleven years ago, shortly after her fifth birthday, from the village of Bihari along the Grass River. Although her resistance to disease, toxins, and radiation would be a great boon as a runner, the church was most interested in her ability to purify a discrete radius of the same substances. Her monthly visits to the king's estate had been part of the Church's tribute to the Kingdom of a Thousand Islands. He skimmed the rest of the paperwork—details about her growth and progress as a runner, a few notices of disciplinary action but nothing alarming, notes regarding the specifics of her abilities, and most recently, the scores from her pathfinder trial. Jackson whistled in appreciation of her performance; although the judges were torn about whether to give her credit for the tenth flag, there was no doubt she passed in any of their tallies.

As the sorcerer returned her file, the inception of a hunch wormed its way into his brain. He moved to another section of archives, those containing the records of his predecessor, a woman of exception abilities named Evelyn. She'd resided at the Monastery of Unseen Waters for twenty years before her death eight years ago when Jackson took the position. She still checked up on him and the monastery from time-to-time from the otherworld; some people don't take retirement well.

Her tight cursive was easy to read and her ledgers neat and precise. He started at the beginning, flipping through years of accounts delineating a steady spirit activity both in the monastery and the ruins—she even battled a fringe shade at one point, losing her left arm in the fight to its time consumption. Not many sorcerers could claim to have survived a run-in with one of those; Jackson made a mental note to remember Evelyn when he got into a jam. As the ledger neared the end, time passed more quickly with progressively fewer and fewer entries—the last three years were little more than the occasional notation, essentially stating: "Nothing to see here."

It could be a coincidence, Jackson thought to himself, *but when it is ever just a coincidence?* Resigned, he returned the ledger and knocked the dust from himself as he left the musty archives.

Chapter Fourteen

The king's estate was bustling with activity: a persistent ebb and flow of lords and vassals, weapons and armor, food and supplies. The wheeze of the blacksmith's bellows continued day and night, and Claudette grumbled about the reduction in her pantry holdings. Khiri knew the signs all too well—Dexter was gearing up for another war. The abbess was relieved that she saw no signs of conflict on their journey there; at least the fighting was nowhere near Unseen Waters, but for how long?

Between the meetings of the war council and Tallis's watchful eye, it was impossible for Khiri to get an audience with Dexter to elicit information. When dinner conversation moved to martial affairs, the king waved his goblet and called for distraction. Fortunately, the king and his guests were well into their cups at the end of her second evening at the estate, granting her a window of opportunity. Make hay when the sun shines.

The tigress walked silently in the deepest shadows, easing her way past the well-oiled study door. Her vision in the dark was exceptional and she examined the maps and pins on the walls and tables without need for light. Dexter's vision, when he took the throne, was to claim as much of Lake Ontario's shore as possible to control trade with the Alliance of Great Canuckistan in the region, but his plans had been less than fruitful.

Currently, Lord King Dexter Albert Winchester VI was at war with no less than three nations, only two with which he shared borders. The Kingdom of a Thousand Islands had lost much of its territory to the Ontario League to the north. To the south, there was the Lordship of Fingers, a nation of octopoid sentients who were originally from the Finger Lakes area but had advanced their borders to encompass the southern shore of Lake Ontario. To the east of Dexter's kingdom were the Rangers of the Adirondack and the Catskill Rangers, and beyond them was the Hudson-Mohawk Demarchy, the third nation with which Dexter was at war.

To be fair, that war wasn't entirely his fault—there had been a diplomatic snafu that precipitated a declaration of war that never officially got revoked. However, when they rebuffed Dexter's entreaties to borrow a warbot in exchange for peace, he doubled down on his aggressions. Khiri surmised that was the purpose of the Oswald reunion. The dowager of the mountain would rather her sons fight the demarchy than each other to establish their separate lands, and the Kingdom of a Thousand Islands needed all the allies it could get.

Perhaps more troubling is why King Dexter VI sought out

a warbot. Located not far from Watertown was Fort Drum, an ancient independent fortification with an automatous defense system. His royal highness reasoned the higher tech that must reside there would turn the tides of battle in his favor— he was a warrior king, and his solution was always bigger weapons— but his last attempt to breech its walls went disastrously.

Khiri scanned the stacks of papers and gleaned the gist of them. The Head Rangers were in alliance in their war against the Hudson-Mohawk Demarchy—there must be some truth in the adage "blood is thicker than water" because Khiri noted no love lost between them at the dinner table last month. However, neither the Rangers of the Adirondack nor the Catskill Rangers were in official alliance with the Kingdom of a Thousand Islands. From the letters Khiri found, Verplanck was unofficially permitting Dexter's troops' passage through their territory and providing guides and scouts through the mountainous terrain for a fee.

Troubled by the increase in hostilities in the region, there was little more Khiri could do about it that night. She was creeping back to her room when she heard a noise from the kitchen. No light shone into the hall, so she doubted it could be Claudette—over the years her squint had become more pronounced and the magnified readers she kept around her neck "just for small print recipes" were now a common feature on her aquiline nose. Khiri came closer to investigate and found Chandi sifting through the pantry and under lids. The abbess knew something was troubling the pathfinder; by this time of night, she should be tucked into her second or third book, well on her way to reading herself to sleep. Khiri cleared her throat ever so slightly and Chandi froze.

"Looking for a late-night snack?" The moonlight reflected in the tigress's pupils.

Chandi straightened up. "My apologies if I woke you, Abbess. I couldn't find the stillness in the night and I thought a snack might help." She could smell the lavender cookies chef had made earlier in the day, but devil if she could find them, even with her low-light vision.

"I daresay between the two of us, we could rustle up something." The tigress's keen sense of smell led her to a different counter where she picked up a lid Chandi had yet to explore. She unearthed a platter of cookies. "There may be some milk or cream from yesterday in the carafe covered with muslin," she suggested as she grabbed two cups from the cupboard. Chandi poured the remainder of the milk and took a seat at the table next to the abbess. She bit into the buttery crumb of the shortbread.

"What troubles you, sister of the stride?" Khiri spoke softly after a moment of silence.

Chandi was unaccustomed to this dynamic. For all the conversations Chandi had with the abbess, there was always another sentient present, either a guard in the carriage or a member of the faculty. Even when she was being doled out punishment, there was always a witness. Chandi wasn't sure how freely to speak, but something in the abbess's tone made her seem less daunting, even in the relative darkness.

"It's about Moonstone," she answered quietly. Khiri replied with silence, nudging the teenager to say more. "If it's causing the trouble…".

"Brothers Jackson and Bartholomew are working diligently to investigate the nature of it. I have every faith they will uncover anything untoward, if there is such a thing to be found," she replied confidently, but the pathfinder seemed to find no solace in the remark. "Is there something else?" She left the question hanging in the air.

"Maybe if I hadn't kept it…" Chandi's voice tapered off.

Khiri waited for more, but none came. "Are you concerned that what has passed is somehow your fault?" she posited.

Chandi took a sip of milk and quoted a tenet of faith. "An attached mind cannot be still. Longing and avarice are types of violence to one's self."

Khiri paused to consider her reply carefully. "A heart that seeks stillness will find its most efficient path, but the true path must be its own."

*****

The spirit paced along the veil, watching the horizon inch nearer and nearer. His anger had run its course for the moment and he looked at the sky of the otherworld; like everything else in here, it was a mere shade of itself. It had been so long since he'd seen the stars as they truly shone. He turned his gaze through the veil, across the narrowing chasm to the other side.

That is my home. I'm coming home.

*****

Jackson nursed another cup of coffee while he and ten guards stood in the main hall just outside of the wards. The brew was no longer warm, but it kept him awake during his vigil. It wasn't that spirit activity happened exclusively at night, but something about the dark seemed to call to the beings of the otherworld. He could hear the voices through the stone more clearly—equal measures of longing, despair, anger, and frustration. He topped off the wards once more; if he was right, they would only have to hold for another twelve hours.

Ariadne entered the hall—sleeping felt too much like surrender and if something was going to attack the monastery, she was going to go down fighting. She took a seat next to the sorcerer and handed him a basket with one of her arms. "A fresh pot from the kitchen, with some bread and cheese." Jackson accepted her peace offering and tore into a hunk of bread. They sat side-by-side, companionable in silence, looking at the small pouch in the center of the room. "Has it said anything else?" she asked.

"More of the same. 'I'm coming home.'" The cadence sent a shiver down Ariadne's body. The sorcerer turned to her. "Thanks for the reinforcements, but there isn't much you can do here tonight. Better for you to get some sleep—morning devotion waits for no one, and you are the one leading tomorrow."

The prioress stubbornly replied, "Ten eyes are better than two." Jackson knew better than to argue; instead, he handed her a cup of hot coffee and a chunk of cheese and bread.

The sun rose over the Monastery of Unseen Waters and its inhabitants continued their daily routine, even in the face of the impending unknown. That was the essence of discipline; it didn't flinch in the face of danger. The prioress was personally reminded of the true meaning of the aphorism when she groggily led morning devotion. Meditations and chores were completed, and she was counting down to the abbess's return. Jackson spent most of the day taking care of minor spirits on the grounds, but continually checked back to the main hall. So far the wards had held. The guards had been rotated but ten kept to their posts. The sorcerer prayed that his luck would hold a little longer, but felt for his dagger and buckle, just in case.

*****

The other side was as close as he had ever seen it, and the abyss that separated him from crossing seemed no more than a large fissure. His mood was almost jovial until it started to expand once more. He knew it was now or never—he would either make it home or fall into oblivion between worlds. Either way, he would no longer be stranded here.

He moved back and took a running leap, piercing the veil headlong, the friction against his ghostly form causing sparks and ripples. A roar erupted as he passed to the other side.

*****

Jackson ran from the other side of the courtyard. He could hear the cacophony of the otherworld and soon he had the spirit's name: Major Tom. He shouted to those milling about to clear out and called the guards to ready when he heard a gut-wrenching wail come from the main hall.

Within the wards appeared a dusty spacesuit bearing the insignia of a nation that had long since died as well. It moved stiffly, the bulk of it hindering free range of motion, but it advanced nonetheless. The visor was raised, but no face graced the awaiting soldiers, just the black void of space. The spacesuit lifted his right hand and a cloud of ash blew out from an unnatural wind. A psychoactive haze filled the room, affecting each sentient differently. Some saw reality bend and flex, taking on unnatural colors they could almost taste. Some began to panic, heart and mind racing in fits of mania and paranoia. Others questioned the meaning of all of this and wondered why the church was so focused on movement—*Why can't we find the stillness in stillness?*

All total, seven of the ten guards were out of commission, either huddled in the fetal position or their bodies limp and their eyes glazed. The spacesuit stepped outside the wards and headed for the main doors to the courtyard. Jackson didn't have time to figure out why the wards hadn't held and instead found the silence within, summoning the pearl of hope. The long-dead sorcerer whispered the words of magic in Jackson's ear and he recited the spell in a strong and commanding tone. The other three guards who kept their feet charged the spirit-made-flesh, piercing its back and flank. A cold blackness spilled out like a fog. Jackson unsheathed his dagger and brought it down, smashing the visor. The sucking vacuum threatened to pull everything inward, but Jackson stood his ground. He spoke to Major Tom in a language only they could understand: "Welcome home, sir."

The blackness swirled around them both and the Order of the Guard dared not stab blindly for fear of hitting Jackson or getting sucked into it themselves. They took defensive stances and waited. From the darkness erupted pinpoints of white, like the brightest stars on the clearest night. The spiral tightened, aiming for Jackson's center. The roar of the wind crescendoed before it petered out as the sorcerer's belt buckle absorbed the last of the darkness and the light.

Jackson lay still; the misery of this spirit took something

with it on its way out. He had all his material parts and pieces, but it would be a while before his spirit would mend. The sorcerer sat up and asked if anyone had a cigarette.

*****

"What the hell did you do to my monastery?!" Khiri demanded as she entered the main hall.

"I'm fine, thanks," Jackson answered. "And no one died, so you're welcome?" He wasn't sure if his cavalier attitude was from sleep deprivation, spiritual injury from the battle with Major Tom, or perhaps he'd inhaled a little of that moon dust.

The abbess walked to one of the pillars, the ward charred. "You broke a ward?!"

"Slight miscalculation on my part. They held great for two nights, but when something that big slides through the veil, it creates a large surge of power. I think it shorted one of the wards and that's how it got loose. Good news is that the sigil is still there, so it's not completely busted, probably just needs some attention and mending. I'll know more once I spend some time on it," Jackson replied casually. Not even the pinpoint pupils of the tigress could harsh his mellow.

Khiri regained her composure before speaking again. "Sister Ariadne, coordinate the clean-up effort. Jackson, in my office now." How the abbess seemed more terrifying when calm was a mystery, to even Jackson.

Chapter Fifteen

"You're sure about this?" the abbess asked Jackson.

"It's a working theory that accounts for the timeline of events," he confirmed.

"But Chandi's not human; she can't hear spirits. How can she have spirit-dampening abilities? The church has no precedent for this kind of ability," Khiri expounded.

"Who looks for the absence of a thing? You only call in a sorcerer when there is spirit activity, not when there seems to be a lack of it," Jackson replied.

She held up Moonstone, "And this?"

"That is something way beyond my pay grade," he commented. "But it I had to make a guess, I would venture that is a lunar meteorite, which is rare in its own right, but this one created a channel from the otherworld of the moon to here."

Khiri blinked twice. "How is that even possible?"

Jackson shrugged. "I don't know how, but it's consistent with everything I've gleaned from the stone and the events so far."

"That can't be. Can't you study it further?"

"Not with Chandi around. That sentient is a spirit dead-zone." This time Jackson completely intended that pun. "When she's nearby, she widens the space between worlds, making it harder for spirits to manifest. It's why the monastery has been relatively light on spirit activity since she arrived."

"And taking it elsewhere to study?"

"Forget about it. You'll have the entire spirit world of the moon looking for a way back to Earth...who knows what kind of specters they have brewing?"

Khiri took to pacing her office. "Is there a way you can test this theory, without blowing up the rest of the monastery or any of its inhabitants?" Jackson looked stumped. Most of his support was sorcerous in nature. Explaining how voices that only he could hear sounded differently around Chandi was hardly going to convince the abbess.

"You willing to sacrifice an ever-lit candle?"

*****

Dinner was filled with chatter. Clearly, something was being stored in the main hall for the past two days, but no one was allowed inside to investigate and there were always guards, not to mention Jackson and the prioress. There weren't many sentients in the courtyard at that time of day as afternoon meditation was finished and most of the evening chores were in the fields, barns, or kitchen. But that didn't stop the speculations. Some heard Jackson had lost an eye, others heard one of the guards went mad and smashed the ward himself. There were multiple variations on the form of the spirit-made-flesh: a marshmallow man, the Michelin Man, or a spacesuit were the top contenders.

Lucy told Chandi about the fight in the courtyard over loose winches, and Willem updated her on the past two days of training with their strange inconsistencies and how Yan got hurt on the course. Chandi took it all in and wasn't sure what to make of it. Could Moonstone be the cause of all this?

Chandi was surprised when the abbess knocked on her door right before bedtime. Lucy gave her a "What did you do?" look to which Chandi answered with a wide-eyed "I have no idea!" Chandi followed Khiri to the main hall where three of the four wards were still operational. *Three is better than none*, the nervous pathfinder reasoned.

Jackson was waiting inside by the busted ward and motioned for them to join him. "Chandi, you don't have to do a thing. Just stand there and I promise, nothing bad is going to happen." Chandi never considered it a good sign when a sentient, especially an adult, felt compelled to make such promises. She nodded politely and waited, with the tigress beside her.

Jackson pulled out an ever-lit candle and uttered the words of unmaking, which sounded like complete gibberish to Chandi and Khiri. He snapped the candle in half and a small fire elemental blinked into view. Khiri gasped—the spirit should have went immediately to the otherworld, not manifested as flesh—and Jackson poked it with his dagger and coaxed it into his belt buckle.

Jackson then walked to the doorway bathed in moonlight and pulled out Moonstone from its pouch. The dull smooth rock looked unimposing in his large calloused hand. He motioned for Chandi to follow and hold her hand out. He placed the meteorite into her palm and it glowed, basking in the moon's rays.

Jackson cast his eyes to Khiri's for recognition. The abbess gave him a slight nod. He picked up Moonstone from the stunned pathfinder's hand and deposited it back into its pouch. "I believe the safest place for this is with you, at least until we know what to do with it in the long term." Jackson handed it to Chandi. "You don't have to carry it everywhere—certainly not even running the local ruins—but just in case, I've secured the mouth of the pouch so it won't slip out. However, it would be best to keep it on your person should you find yourself traveling, say to the king's estate on a tribute visit."

Chandi took Moonstone; its weight seemed heavier to her now. Khiri bowed and nodded to Chandi, bidding her stillness in the night. The abbess didn't have to tell Chandi not to tell anyone about Moonstone—her intent gaze told Chandi as much. The pathfinder stashed it in the inner pocket of her pants and headed back to her room.

"Well?" Lucy needled Chandi as soon as she closed the door on her return.

"She took me to the main hall. Jackson broke a candle and handed me a rock," Chandi reported just the facts; she knew if she tried to lie to Lucy, she would suss it out immediately. Chandi pulled on her nightclothes and blew out of the light.

"A rock?" Lucy puzzled.

"Yeah, it was weird." Chandi definitely wasn't lying about that part. "But they cleaned up the main hall, so looks like morning devotion won't be outdoors anymore." She nestled under her covers. Even though the night was warm, she sought the comfort of her blanket. She held the pouch in her hand, waiting for Lucy to sleep before stashing away in her hiding place.

Lucy yawned. "Pity. I kinda liked it."

*****

The last of the robed elders entered the smoke-filled chamber and a spin of the prayer wheel marked the beginning of their meeting. There were many pieces of business to discuss, some procedural, others state affairs, but at the end of the docket was something called "Moonstone."

The senior steward led the council of thirteen and motion after motion was made and seconded. They reviewed new church business and deliberated the appropriate course of action. Lastly, a delegate speaking on behalf of the Unseen Waters took the floor.

"It has come to the attention of this delegate that an item of some power has fallen from the sky and is now in possession at the Monastery of Unseen Waters. The local sorcerer there has run initial tests and believes it to be a spiritual link to the otherworld of the moon. Brother Jackson is petitioning the council for guidance on how to proceed with such an item, as well as resources to create a containment vessel that will allow its safe transport away from the monastery for further study."

The item raised eyebrows and voices alike. A single figure lowered her hood and raised a slender hand, quieting the kerfuffle. "Perhaps I could be of some service in this discussion," Cassandra spoke in a neutral tone. "Such an item would be invaluable, both to research as well as mining for resources. The entire spirit realm of the moon has been untapped until now."

"Which is why it must be destroyed!" a vociferous voice asserted. "Perhaps smash it or melt it down to its component parts—that should sever the lunar link."

"Or open the portal wide," another suggested. "You can't reason with sorcery, no offense intended." He nodded to Cassandra. She accepted his qualifier with a semi-formal bow.

"None taken, but the esteemed brother is correct. We have no idea what the result would be if we attempt to destroy it."

A quivering warble offered her suggestion. "Didn't we make

a containment vessel once? Why couldn't we put it in there?"

"Because it is currently occupied," another elder answered curtly.

"You can't put two items in the same box? Maybe put a partition between them?" another inquired. All eyes turned to Cassandra, the only sorcerer in the room.

"My venerable sister of the stride makes an illuminating point. It is certainly possible, but given the item that is already contained in the vessel, it may not be altogether advisable," she countered diplomatically.

"Remind us what's in the containment box again?"

"The dragon's tooth." A quiet hush fell over the room. "You can see the cause for concern. Having a spiritual conduit from the moon talking to the wyrm's remains seems an unnecessary risk."

"How long will it take to make such a container?"

Although she had done the math before the meeting even took place, Cassandra paused for effect. "The first vessel took years to complete, but now that we know how to make it and what materials and spirits would be required, that significantly shortens production time. If the council made it priority, we could probably finish it in six months." Everyone stared, awed at the estimate—six months certainly sounded much better than years.

A shrewd council member who had yet to speak added his voice to the conversation. "How has Unseen Waters contained

Moonstone up until now?"

"As I understand it, they have a pathfinder who is training there with the ability to suppress spirit manifestation. That, in combination with some creative uses of the spirit wards, has minimized damage." The elders in the room clearly didn't know what to make of the sorcerer's revelation.

"Would it be possible to use Moonstone in the meantime to further our diplomatic work? It will take six months to build an appropriate vessel; why let it sit inside a monastery where no one can benefit from its presence?" The suggestion was appealing, but no one wanted to be the first to start naming names.

"Isn't the monastery in Watertown? Have we found a suitable replacement for the warmonger? What kind of mad king goes to war with a non-adjacent nation?" one councilwoman suggested.

"Unfortunately, his cousin is still too young to claim the throne outright and his guardian is not much better than Dexter."

"Plus," Cassandra added, "it would be unwise to deposit such an item in a kingdom with such a strong cadre of sorcerers at their disposal. We risk losing the item altogether if it is found—all knowledge and resources it could offer would be mined by another." The council collectively agreed with this observation.

The shrewd voice in the back spoke once more. "The

Lordship of the Fingers has rebuffed our emissary for a third time. The octopoids are a xenocentric race—they would hardly have a stable of sorcerers on hand. If I recall, their territory isn't far from the Monastery of Unseen Waters." The chamber hummed with consideration of the notion. "This pathfinder of theirs, is he a true believer?"

"She has been in at the monastery for over a decade in service to the church," Cassandra deftly corrected the elder councilman. "She is still in training, but shows great promise. Perhaps a personal visit to the monastery to deliver the council's decisions is in order to assess the situation firsthand."

The steward officially proposed the motion, another seconded, and Cassandra left to pack her bags.

Chapter Sixteen

"It was a full moon," Indra began once her daughter had washed her face and sat down to have her hair brushed.

"Just like tonight," the young girl interjected, pointing to the bright cluster of the fractured moon out the window.

"Yes, and the wind was still and the evening quiet. Even the animals knew better than disrupt that night." She started at the ends and moved up the silky black tresses. "Your father was out hunting and running late, but you had different ideas. You were coming early." Indra worked out the knots, and the child fidgeted under her mother's firm hand as it steadied itself against her head.

"Were you scared?" she squeaked.

"A little," her mother admitted. "But I was also excited to finally see you."

"Then what happened?" she asked, more from habit than curiosity. It was their nightly ritual: a story while her mother minded her hair. She had heard this tale many times; the story of her birth was one of her favorites.

"I was admiring the bright light in the sky when I felt

the water fall between my legs. That's when I knew you were coming." With all the tangles smoothed, she divided her girl's hair into sections and began weaving.

"Did it hurt?" the little girl whispered. She intuitively lowered her voice when speaking of unpleasant things, but felt compelled to ask nonetheless; she was always inquisitive.

"Of course," her mother replied. "Life must fight its way into being." Her daughter nodded her head in agreement. "Stop squirming or the braid will be loose and fall out," Indra chided. "But it didn't hurt long because you were ready to leave, and soon, I had you wrapped in my arms." She twisted the strands reflexively. "I cleaned you off with water drawn from the river and I counted your fingers."

"All ten of them!" she responded, wiggling her outstretched digits.

"And I counted your toes."

"Five on each side!" She giggled. Chandi was always good with call and response.

"Yes, five on each side," her mother mollified her. "And your first cries of life called your father home. He held you in the light of the full moon." Indra heard a knock at the cottage door. She secured the ends of the braid with a tie. "And that's when we gave you your name, bathed in the moonlight and the fresh waters of the river. Chandini." She heard her husband answer the door and muffled voices from the other room. She knew she didn't have much time.

She turned her daughter around by the shoulders. "You will remember, won't you? Remember your parents knew what a blessing you were from the first beginning?" Her eyes were wide open, searching for comprehension.

Chandi's green eyes met her mother's, calm and loving. "I will remember, Momma," she promised.

Her mother unfastened a chain around her neck and secured the too-large necklace around the young girl's neck, tucking the lotus pendent under her clothes. "You won't forget?"

"Never." Her daughter crossed her heart. Indra clasped Chandi's small frame in her arms.

The door opened upon them and Chandi saw her father's silhouette in the doorway with a figure behind him. "It's time," was all he said.

Chandi broke from her mother's embrace and put her short arms around her father's waist. "Don't worry, Papa. I won't forget."

"I know, Chandi. Such a clever girl." He sighed wistfully, with one hand on her back and the other patting her head, careful not to disrupt his wife's handiwork.

The figure appeared from behind her father, dressed in flowing black robes. She pulled back her hood, revealing striped fur on her face and hands. The visitor crouched beside the young girl. "Greetings, Chandi. I'm Khiri, a sister of the stride. Are you ready to go?"

Chandi took one last look around the cottage and mustered

her courage with an exaggerated deep breath. She straightened her shoulders and put her hand into the tigress's outstretched palm. The pair were about to step into the ephemeral nothingness beyond the door when Chandi woke up, clutching the lotus pendent with one hand and the Moonstone with the other. Only after she ensured that both were where they should be did Chandi take a breath.

She had been having similar dreams all week: visions of home. Sometimes they were memories, like tonight's; other times, they were projection into a past that didn't happen, like playing with her younger sister, whom she had never met. Sometimes they were reminiscent scenes, other times deeply saddening. On the whole, they were throwing Chandi off-balance, a precarious position for both a runner and the bearer of the Moonstone. She had spent most of her life at the Monastery of Unseen Waters, with only the occasional nostalgic dream. She had kept her promise and never forgot where she came from and who she was before she became a seeker of the true path, but never had her dreams weighed so heavy on her spirit. They weren't nightmares, per se, but they weren't happy, either.

An immediate return to daily life was Khiri's solution to disruption. There was resiliency in ritual and in a way, routine constituted its own rite: the sun rises, everyone sits in stillness together, the porridge is hot and plentiful, and the day goes on. What we do is what we do.

Once everyone saw that Jackson had indeed kept both his eyes and the physical signs of disorder had been cleared away or mended, the rampant speculations of what exactly happened in the main hall that day before dinner eventually died down. After all, that was a perk of training with the Church of Parkour—the ability to return to habit in relative safety was a luxury in and of itself in the chaotic world under the shattered moon.

But the solace that most found in routine escaped Chandi; she was left with more questions than answers. She tacitly accepted her role as Moonstone's keeper. As long as she kept it near her, everyone else was safe—that was the important thing for now. Even though Jackson told her she didn't have to carry it on her person while she was near the monastery, she felt better knowing where it was at all times. When it was hidden in her stash, she continually checked on it, and it simply became easier to wear it all the time. The only time Moonstone was separate from Chandi was when she left it with Jackson while she ran the ruins; even that was at the sorcerer's behest, since it was the only time the pathfinder was far enough away from the meteorite for him to hear a tidbit of the lunar otherworld's conversations.

Chandi couldn't hear Moonstone the same way that Jackson could, but she suspected her recent nightly dreams were its attempts to communicate with her. It started out innocently enough one morning, when the aroma of incense during morning devotion conjured images of the small shrine in her parents' home where they still paid reverence to the old gods— her mother, Vishnu, and her father, Ganesha. Then one day, the warm and filling pottage that she had eaten daily for lunch for over a decade suddenly tasted bland compared to the fried bits of battered vegetables and chaat that graced her parents' table. Eventually, she took to wearing her mother's pendent, which she typically secreted to prevent possible confiscation, but what was that risk when she was carrying around a conduit to the moon around her waist? And then the dreams started.

Chandi wasn't sure why Moonstone was showing her these things. Was it even deliberate, or just a consequence of being in near proximity of such melancholy? If it was purposeful, was it trying to elicit empathy for their cause? They just wanted to come home…didn't everyone want to be home? Or was it punishment for stalling their homecoming? If so, it was a necessary burden until Jackson heard word from the elder council about requested aid. While their motivations may not seem sinister, their presence made-flesh was rarely innocuous, from what Chandi had heard.

The pathfinder had always accepted her dharma—she was given a gift and she went where she was needed—but for the first time in her brief life, she wondered where *she* needed to be and if that was even an appropriate question to ask. Lucy's soft snore broke her train of thought, and Chandi reluctantly closed her eyes, hoping for stillness in what remained of the night.

*****

Jackson hastily donned his kit and pulled up his boots on his way out of the door. It was partially his fault—he should have kept up on his correspondence instead of letting it pile up on his desk—but he also blamed all the extra work he was doing repairing the ward and examining Moonstone when Chandi ran the ruins. He never expected the elder council to reply so quickly, and he certainly didn't anticipate them sending Cassie to deliver the news. With any luck, he'd be in the ruins with the Order of the Guard when she arrived at the monastery, there would be a perfunctory meeting with the abbess that might or might not require his presence, and she would be on her way tomorrow. After all, Cassie was a busy woman and surely he could make it through one meeting and a communal dinner, right?

He hustled and joined a squad of guards assigned to monitor the ruins. They seemed glad for his company—word of the strange spirit activity within Unseen Water's walls had saturated the ranks and in their minds, the ruins were always safer with a sorcerer. They trekked over broken concrete, defunct masonry, and partially standing structures all morning and afternoon, taking a light lunch in between. The heat of summer was starting to relent, hinting that fall would arrive before long.

*****

For most under the shattered moon, summer was traditionally a lean time when winter larders were at a low and sentients waited for crops to mature for harvest. Animals were still nursing their young, the grazing was thinning out, and those intended for slaughter needed fattening. Fortunately, the Church of Parkour provided those in their service—which included the Order of the Guard—more than enough food for three square meals a day. However, the residents of the ruins were not so lucky.

It is said that hunger makes the best sauce, that hunger steals the memory, that hunger never saw bad bread, and that hunger knows no friend but its feeder. It stands to reason that hunger was the driving force behind the rat's bold probe into the pool of glowing green goo. Under different circumstances, the rat would have investigated the puddle before consuming— perhaps something in its smell or initial taste would have turned it off. Even the simplest of sentients knew to steer clear of luminous green fluid and recognized the telltale circular symbol for radioactive material, but the rat didn't have the benefit or hindrance of intelligence—it was a being of impulse and it was famished.

Rather than kill the creature outright, its poisonous meal only wetted its appetite and devoured what little caution it had.

Inextricable changed, the rat roamed the nooks and crannies in the rubble for more food. Sensing movement, the rabid rodent went in for the kill, sinking its sharp teeth into flesh. Its quarry was exponentially larger and merely let out a curse as he unceremoniously impaled the rat with his spear. The guard washed out the wound and shook his hand dry before joining Jackson and the rest of the squad as they headed back to base.

Chapter Seventeen

The flag of the Church of Parkour fluttered in the wind as the horses trotted across the countryside. The carriage hit another bump in the road, jostling its inhabitants once more. Cassandra glanced up from her paperwork toward Hinkley, the tinker sitting opposite her. When the sorcerer recommended visiting the Monastery of Unseen Waters, she hadn't intended on being saddled with company, but the elder council had spoken—they wanted technological support on this operation. If Moonstone was legitimate, they didn't want to lose sight of it and insisted on marking it with UV paint, which Cassandra could have done herself no matter how distasteful she found it, but she wasn't going anywhere near the UV light required to confirm it was done. Thus, Hinkley's presence was a necessary compromise.

It's not that Cassandra had anything against him personally or against tinkers in general. On the contrary, she considered herself unconventional in most of her opinions, but technology was one area where she was a strict traditionalist. She acknowledged the tinker's role and usefulness in the church, she just didn't want to be in proximity of anything higher-tech than say that from the ancient's eighteenth century. Bad things happened to sorcerers who played with technology; those who tried to know both sorcery and super-science paid with their sanity. Like most sorcerers under the shattered moon, Cassandra chose complete avoidance whenever possible. It was the only way to be sure. She breathed a sigh of relief as they entered the ruins of Watertown; it wouldn't be long until she could leave her confinement—forced by the necessity of travel—mere feet and inches away from the tinker's kit.

Returning to Unseen Waters was a homecoming of sorts for Cassandra, who'd apprenticed under the former resident sorcerer. When she wasn't learning the ins and outs of the otherworld from Evelyn, Cassie was running. Technically, she never advanced beyond novice, but it wasn't from lack of trying: the church felt it unwise to "waste" a sorcerous resource on running the ruins when they could clearly "run" in the otherworld. In hindsight, she acknowledged that it was probably for the best, and she had done well for herself as otherworld advisor to the elder council, but there was a freedom in movement that could not be attained in drafting statements and steering policy.

As they pulled up to the front gates, the Order of the Guard stopped the carriage to confirm their identity and purpose. As the carriage slowly pulled within the walls, Cassie saw the abbess was there to greet her, along with her arachnid prioress. She noted Jackson's absence as she disembarked from her transport.

Khiri extended her old friend a formal greeting befitting her position and fought the urge to call her "Cassie," a moniker from Cassandra's youth, used by intimate associates. Had it really been so many years since they were mere kids, unburdened with the mantle of responsibility their respective stations endowed? The tigress turned her attention to the sorcerer's absentminded companion, a lanky sentient with more pockets on his vest and pants than she would have thought possible. When the abbess received the elder council's message of an envoy consisting of both a sorcerer *and* tinker, she figured it was an act of utter unawareness or malice. Knowing the council, it could be either or both.

"Welcome to the Monastery of Unseen Waters. I hope your journey was not too taxing." Khiri's eyes shifted briefly to Hinkley before catching Cassie's. "Unfortunately, Brother Jackson is away performing his duties, otherwise I'm sure he wouldn't miss the opportunity to greet you himself." All three sisters of the stride shared a silent moment, reflecting on how vexing the resident sorcerer could be in their experience. "In the meantime, we have rooms ready for each of you and a late lunch, as it will be some time before dinner. Your guards will find food and accommodations with the Order of the Guard. There will be plenty of time to hear the council's wisdom later today when all associated parties are present and available."

Everyone exchanged bows before retreating to their

designated sanctuaries.

*****

Jackson turned the key in his lock, only to find that it was already open. He figured his intruder was not spiritual in nature; in his experience, ghosts don't need to pick locks to get in. He cautiously pulled out his dagger—it wasn't only dangerous to otherworldly beings—before nudging the door open.

"If I didn't know better, I would say you were avoiding me."

Jackson instantly recognized that resonant tone heavily laced with sarcasm. He sheathed his dagger; it wouldn't help him with this encounter. "Cassie—when did you start breaking into other people's room?" Jackson parried back without missing a beat.

"When said persons are too chicken-shit to greet an old friend." Cassie sipped at the amber liquid in her tumbler. A second glass was waiting on the table with the chair opposite her already drawn.

"Is that what we are?" Jackson unloaded his kit and accepted a seat in his own room. "Help yourself, by the way…" He knocked back the generous double she had already poured him.

"You always had the best whisky. Some things never

change." The rhythm of their patter fell into step. Jackson recalled that had never been their problem.

"Why don't we save the trip down memory lane, and you just tell me why you are here?" Jackson cut straight to the point.

She leaned forward and a hint of liquor carried with her husky voice. "At the monastery or in your room?" Jackson gave her a sardonic stare until she realized he was going to be no fun at all. "I'm here to deliver the council's decision," she answered curtly and sat back. Jackson poured himself another.

"A letter would have sufficed," he noted. She took another sip before pushing the empty glass away and recomposed herself in her seat.

"If Moonstone is what you say it is—"

"It is."

She cut her eyes at him before continuing. "Then surely you understand the council's need for verification in their plans."

A burst of laughter escaped from deep in his gut. "Cassie, anyone with half a brain and a decent pair of eyes knows the council's plans are whatever you want them to be when it comes to all things otherworldly."

Cassie failed to fully suppress her smile and brushed an errant brunette lock from her face. "Even if that were true, I wouldn't be doing my due diligence without examining it."

"Good luck with that when Chandi's around—might as well be any old rock if she's inside the monastery walls. She's got to be at least a hundred meters into the ruins before I even hear a whisper out of Moonstone."

Cassie's ears perked up at the mention of the pathfinder trainee. "Yes, I'd like to meet her. How did you figure out her special abilities?"

Jackson shrugged. "Did some research in the archives, put some timelines side-by-side until I saw a pattern, and ran some preliminary tests. It didn't hurt that the thing lit up in her hands in the moonlight."

Cassie gazed in awe at her companion. "You've been doing your homework."

Jackson grinned. "Don't tell anyone—I'd hate to ruin my bad reputation."

"And your opinion about how she does it?"

Jackson paused to choose his words carefully—it was better to be precise with someone like Cassie. "I think her presence creates a metaphysical gap between the two worlds so that simply passing through the veil is no longer enough for a spirit to be made flesh in this world."

Cassie raised an eyebrow. "Do you think she could control it?"

Jackson didn't like the direction the conversation was taking. "Probably not. Her other abilities are innate; she can't turn them off or otherwise exert any control over them, and initial attempts by the church to expand her radius on her other auras have been unfruitful." Cassie looked slightly crestfallen, which he took as a sign in Chandi's favor.

"Well, I'm here and I'd like to examine it tonight. Can you arrange for Pathfinder Choudary to meet me after dinner with Moonstone and for her to leave the monastery—far enough so I have an hour or two with it?"

Jackson spelled out her request in plain terms, "You want to send a pathfinder trainee into the ruins at night for an hour or two?"

Cassie waved her hand flippantly in the air. "Well, obviously not alone. You can accompany her, as well as some of the Order of the Guards."

Jackson wobbled his head noncommittally. Cassie never had a problem delegating work to others. "You ran this by the abbess?"

"I'm sure the mother of the stride will see reason in such a request," she replied nonplussed; she was a woman used to getting things done her way.

*****

Chandi knew she was being sized up, but she didn't know what for. Sister Cassandra's gaze was intent, her questions thorough, and her manner a little too friendly. And then there was the way the abbess and Jackson watched her instead of Chandi or Moonstone. The visiting sorcerer didn't seem surprised when Moonstone glowed in Chandi's hand, although Hinkley was more than a little intrigued. Chandi noticed the wide birth both Jackson and Cassandra gave the tinker, as if getting too close to him was perilous, but Chandi could hardly imagine this mild-mannered, soft-spoken, unassuming sentient could be dangerous...until she saw the weapon holstered under his arm.

Chandi left Moonstone with the abbess and the monastery's visitors while she and Jackson headed into the ruins with a squad of guards. Jackson knew his presence wasn't needed for protection from the spirit world with Chandi around, but he wouldn't send anyone into the ruins alone after dark. Everyone under the shattered moon knew that ruins could be hazardous at any time, but especially in the evening.

Chandi had never been in the ruins at night. Officially, the church strongly advised against nocturnal running. There was a protocol for septs that got stranded overnight in the ruins, but they hadn't yet covered that in training. She was simultaneously excited and anxious. Even with her excellent vision in low light, the outlines of rubble and their cast shadows seemed darker and more menacing, the noises more acute and startling, and the late summer air cooler than its actual temperature.

Once the Order of the Guard ushered Jackson and Chandi about a hundred meters out from the monastery walls, they established a perimeter patrol. Jackson parked himself on a comfortable slab of plascrete that was still radiating the day's warmth; he had inspected the area during the day and had survived worse things than nighttime. Chandi paced within the order's perimeter; she didn't know how to be physically still in a place that was always meant to be run.

"Take a seat kid, or you'll wear out the rubble," Jackson commented after a few minutes. Chandi sat on her heels to his side, but not so near to be considered beside him; Chandi had a healthy respect and subsequent suspicion of the otherworld and those that could communicate with it and command it. She folded her hands around her bent legs.

"Do you think she'll take it with her?" Chandi queried nearly into her knees.

"Maybe, but I wouldn't count on it." Her exhale of resignation was almost palpable. Jackson's brow rose. He didn't want to ask, but he knew he was supposed to. "Everything all right, Chandi? With Moonstone, I mean."

She shuffled her weight on her feet. "You can hear it, right? When I'm running out here?"

"Yeah."

Chandi rotated to face him. "What does it say?"

Jackson leaned back. "Well, it's not so much that the rock says anything. It's like a giant funnel, channeling a bunch of voices. It's a jumble of noise that starts off quiet but gets louder, mostly talking about being able to cross over into our world."

"Are they mad at me?" He could see the moonlight glint in her green eyes.

"I don't know that they even know you exist, just that conditions fluctuate. The more hope they have of crossing over and then fail, they more emotional they get. Sometimes they are angry, sometimes they're sad; other times, it's abject nihilism."

"Nihilism?"

"No matter what you do or don't do, it doesn't matter. Nothing that ever existed or will exist means anything," he clarified bluntly.

Chandi nodded and quoted a tenet of faith, "The only true path is perfect stillness. All others are a false hope."

Jackson cracked a sideways smile. "I'm a little rusty on my scripture, but in my experience, the only thing worse than not getting what you want is *almost* getting it."

The pathfinder considered his words but her mood did not lighten. Even though Moonstone was still inside Unseen Waters, she could feel the weight of it, like an amputee that still perceives their missing limb.

"Do you think it could communicate to sentients other than sorcerers?" Chandi wondered.

"I think that some sentients are very sensitive to latent energy and such individuals have to take care to shield themselves from negative forces," Jackson replied diplomatically. "Misery loves company."

"But if they just want to go home and I'm keeping them from returning. Aren't I the bad guy, from their perspective?"

Jackson's demeanor turned grim as he squared his shoulders and looked at Chandi straight on. "This isn't their world. They have no more right to it. Never forget that." Chandi suddenly understood why the spirits of the otherworld obeyed his command.

*****

Khiri pulled out two glasses as Cassie produced a bottle of wine from her copious robes. It had been a long night and both women could use a drink. They had known each other long enough that a few nods and hand gestures were sufficient to coordinate the pouring.

"Your thoughts?" the abbess broke the silence after their first sip.

Cassie sat back and pulled her legs under her. "The wine is nice."

The tigress screwed her face into a smirk. "You know what I mean, Cassie."

The brunette sighed. "As much as I hate to admit it, Jackson was right."

The light in Khiri's eyes danced with amusement, but she didn't laugh out loud or make comment. Instead, she asked, "So the elder council will assist?"

"Yes, but it will take time to make something that can contain it. Six months is the best I can do." Cassie swirled the burgundy elixir in the glass.

Khiri leaned back and looked over her drink. "And?"

"You are just as suspicious as Jackson!" Cassie exclaimed defensively.

Khiri laughed so softly, it almost came out like a purr. "That doesn't mean I'm wrong."

Cassie shook her head side-to-side petulantly; that was the problem negotiating with sentients that knew you too well. "The council is considering using Moonstone to further its diplomatic reach in the region, especially considering the political climate," she admitted reluctantly. "It would be unwise to rely solely on a king who might lose one of these wars he's fighting."

"And how, pray tell, would the elders like to proceed?" the abbess momentarily indulged this flight of fancy.

Cassie finished her first glass and poured herself another while offering to top off Khiri's glass. The tigress abstained. "It was suggested that Pathfinder Choudary could deposit Moonstone in the Lordship of Fingers's territory to help open relations."

"So you want to haunt their land, help them clear the ghosts, and come out as an ally?" Khiri summed up.

"You make it seem so sinister," Cassie dismissed her old friend. "It's not like we haven't tried more conventional diplomatic means, but they are stalwart in their refusal. We are just prodding them in the right direction."

Khiri placed her glass down on her desk once she realized Cassie was serious. "Absolutely not. She's just a trainee and that kind of distance would involve a multiday run."

"What if we could limit it to an overnight run and we ran her with a sept of tracers?" Cassie never went into a negotiation blind. She had double and triple checked the math on the way down. Oswego was on the edge of the octopoids' territory and far enough from their main base at Syracuse for any serious patrolling. It would allow Chandi and the tracers to use a transport for much of the distance both coming in and going out, minimizing their nights in the ruins.

Khiri scrutinize the sorcerer across from her. "The elder council has approved such resources?"

"If the council agreed to such measures, would you consider it a possibility?" Cassie's impassive mien didn't falter. "It would bring great favor to Unseen Waters."

"I'm not throwing one of the most promising runners that has come through this monastery to the bunnysharks for a little social cache with the elder council," Khiri replied emphatically.

Cassie softened her tone and her countenance. "Have you considered asking Chandi if she would like to do it? Take it from someone who was told it was in everyone's best interest if she didn't run—it sucks not to be asked, even if your answer is the same in the end."

Khiri accepted a second glass as considered her friend's words. The full-bodied wine had a pleasantly fruity and spiced aroma. It really was a nice wine.

Chapter Eighteen

Why is it so hot? Emer thought to himself as he shifted once more in his damp bedclothes while avoiding putting pressure on his injured hand; it was exquisitely tender to the slightest touch despite the padding of the bandage. He wasn't one to visit the infirmary, but as the site of the bite got more swollen and hot, with a throbbing pain that ebbed and flowed with each heartbeat, he'd relented and let them wash it out, cover it with salve, and wrap it.

It wasn't a particularly warm night, but his febrile state made it a long one, waking every few hours drenched in the hopes that this time, the fever had broken for good. By the morning, he was wan and exhausted, but he was never one to shirk his duties. The ruins needed patrolling and Emer donned his gear.

His squad was eight strong, a few soldiers short due to shuttling sentients back and forth from the monastery. The Order of the Guard patrolled different sections of the ruins each day, clearing any individual swath on a weekly basis. The banter was par for the course that morning: someone was too ugly for words, another had a promiscuous sister or a fat mother, others had some slight habit or affectation that could be mercilessly exploited for laughs. Busting each other's chops was as close to a team-building exercise as the order got, but they expressed genuine concern when they picked up on their leader's poorly state, even though it was met with disregard. Emer wasn't going to let a rat bite put him out of commission.

Emer led his squad due south in the early morning light and ordered his soldiers to cut down the chatter and keep a watchful eye on the ruins. They spread out in formation, spears ready and pointed outward for whatever lay ahead of them in the debris. They advanced, watching and listening for movement. As they moved further into the rubble, the air became stale and heavy as the sun rose in the sky and burned away the last of the cool dew that lingered.

Emer felt the flush return as beads of perspiration collected on his brow. He felt a heaviness in his chest and a dull ache in the back of his skull. The pain quickly spread across his entire head, intensifying into a sharp stabbing sensation. As he fell to the ground, his whole body convulsed, limbs akimbo. Those closest to him broke formation first, taking a knee beside their downed squad leader. Someone barked orders for the remaining four guards to secure a perimeter while white foam frothed out of Emer's mouth. His eyes rolled back into his head and his breath was ragged, deep, and fast. His chest arched and twisted off the ground as if it was being rung out by an invisible hand.

His comrades hoped for the best once the shaking had

stopped; the ruins had become quiet and still once more. The three guards beside Emer removed his helmet to assess the damage and were reassured that he was still breathing. They had just loosened his armor to let him breathe easier when his eyelids fluttered and suddenly opened wide. His pinpoint pupils darted frantically. An unearthly roar escaped from Emer's lips as a pair of chitinous insectoid legs erupted from his sides.

Those beside him could see the roiling undulation under his clothes as his skin hardened into an exoskeleton and piles of plascrete formed a carapace. His fingers elongated into talons, rending the flesh of a one of his nearby companions. As one soldier slammed his blade forward toward Emer's stomach, the plascrete disk on Emer's back moved to his belly, deflecting the blow. Emer's face contorted and his mouth widened into a gaping maw that bit into his attacker's thigh. Warm sanguine effluvium pulsated from the severed femoral artery.

The third sentient kneeling beside him decided to flee, only he could not outrun the arch of electricity shooting from Emer's elongated index fingers. The smell of burnt flesh filled the air; it made the creature smile. In that moment, the last essence of Emer vanished and its transformation was complete. It was now a being of the ruins and it was hungry.

It leapt on its four legs and made quick work of the remaining four guards who fought as valiantly as they could. The tattered shreds of the Church of Parkour flag dangled from what was once Emer's chest as the groue horror that had taken his form bound deeper into the ruins.

*****

The pathfinder trainees prepared for their run: stretching their bodies, securing laces and ties, and tightening straps on their packs. They were moving deeper into Watertown's ruins with the promise of new obstacles and scavenged finds. Ever since Chandi became Moonstone's official keeper, she grew increasingly fond of her runs, where she was free of the stone's yoke and managed to find the stillness that eluded her otherwise as of late. She yearned for movement and relished the clarity of thought that came to her in those moments.

Netu set the pace with Bibi bringing up the rear. They silently flowed over the landscape as a troop: leaping, crawling, jumping, and sprinting. Chandi's muscles started to warm and loosen. Out of the corner of her eye, she could see Jukka's sylvan form swing over uneven ground. She felt Mira and Natalie glide past her to her left. Joshi and Willem kept pace on either side of her while Finn and Yan were somewhere behind her. There was an ease to their coordinated migration through the remains of Watertown; nary a collision or awkward near miss struck the sept. Chandi basked in this moment of zen.

They were just about to enter a clearing when she heard Netu make a bird's call and saw him throw up a hand signal to halt and hide. The pathfinders ceased their migration and found the deepest darkness nearest them, ears and eyes perked for signs of danger. The ruins seemed still and quiet, but none dared to take a step out of the shadows until either Netu or Bibi gave the all clear. Netu picked up a rock and hurled it on the far side; time stretched as the rattle of its descent to the ground ended in a firm plunk, but nothing stirred. The black lines from Netu's skin leeched out and Umbra appeared. Its long legs made short work of the span to the clearing, engaging its extraordinary senses and prodding the rubble as it went.

As Umbra came upon a pile of plascrete, the scritch hissed and adopted a defensive posture. The debris moved and the groue horror rose to its full height of seven feet, towering over the otherwise giant tarantula. Netu gave the signal to run as Umbra shot out a stream of poisonous spit from its mouth before retreating. Bibi led the flight back to the monastery walls while Netu and his scritch covered the pathfinder's retreat. The groue horror's howl let everyone know Umbra's aim was true, but none risked the fraction of a second to look back.

The groue horror salivated at the prospect of so many prey despite the ulcerated skin from Umbra's poison. The edges of the lesion were already secreting a foul glowing-green liquid, narrowing the gash and quickly sealing the wound. Fully healed in less than a second, the groue horror began his hunt in earnest.

The pathfinders could hear the lumbering gait of the creature pursuing them, the click of its four chitinous legs ricocheting through the ruins. Each runner picked up their pace and the formation lost its cohesion as discipline and coordination slowly unraveled in the face of fear. They all knew the ruins were dangerous, but this was the first time they felt it—whatever was behind them desired to kill them. Willem and Joshi kept pace with Chandi while Jukka, Mira, and Natalie caught up and Yan and Finn fell back. Bibi made a path for the gates of the monastery while Netu and Umbra did their best to slow down the menace. It wasn't much further to the safety of the walls—if only they could keep running.

The groue horror raged at the prospect of losing all of its prey and changed tactics. Rather than trying to outrun them, it would sabotage their retreat. The monster nimbly scaled a mound of rubble and hurled its body against a precarious stack. The avalanche of debris echoed through the once-suburban peaks and valleys, abruptly changing the landscape. All the runners were well ahead of the obstacle except for Finn, Yan, Netu, and Umbra. Chandi chanced a quick glance over her shoulder and caught a glimmer of Finn's iridescent scales crest the rocky bank, followed by Netu and Umbra. Netu abandoned all attempts of stealth and yelled for the pathfinders to pick up the pace. Chandi pushed harder but looked back once more to see Yan's petite figure clear the mound with the groue horror close on her tail. Yan was running oddly, avoiding pressure on her right side.

She's injured; she isn't going to make it, Chandi thought to herself. Without a moment's hesitation, Chandi heard Willem's objection as she broke from the pack and circled back for Yan. She grabbed a handful of rocks and waited for Yan to pass before pelting the groue horror and attracting its ire toward herself. Once Chandi got its attention, she took off at a fifteen-degree angle from the sept, followed by the aggravated horror. If Chandi's thinking was correct, Bibi would lead the sept to the front gates and her trajectory should lead to the Order of the Guard, where there is always someone patrolling their fortifications and the nearby ruins.

The clicking of its insectoid legs was Chandi's metronome—as long as her pace was faster than that, she would make it to safety. As she neared the order's perimeter, the erratic staccato of musket and rifle fire was music to Chandi's ears, but it did not stop the relentless pursuit of the horror whose plascrete disk deftly moved around its body to deflect the bullets without injury. Chandi gazed up the twenty-foot monastery walls, something she had always seen as a limitation but now understood was also protection. She could hear the peel of a bell—Bibi had gotten back to the monetary and raised the alarm. The sept couldn't be far behind her.

Chandi spied a corner she could ascend and raced toward it, building as much forward momentum as possible. She planted one foot after another on the masonry, springing up the wall until she reached the top. Once on top, Chandi assessed her landing options while the gunfire intensified from below—the perimeter guards had called for reinforcements within the fort. The groue horror roared and for a moment, Chandi locked eyes with her pursuer and saw raw rage and destruction in its elongated plasticine face. Chandi leapt from the wall and her outstretched arms led the way as she curled her body for a double roll twenty feet below into the uninhabited rows of the herb garden.

The groue horror paid no mind to the bullets as its innate plascrete shield moved to block each projectile. It was focused on more interesting things, like the tasty morsel that had dropped behind the wall. The creature backed up and made a running jump for the wall; the impact of its carapace reverberated throughout the monastery. The soldiers aimed for its posterior and again the plascrete disk granted it immunity. The horror wedged its arms and legs into a corner and started shimming up when a panel opened from the top of the wall, exposing a slim barrel tipped by a red light. Three bolts of plasma cut through the horror from stem to stern, its disturbing bellow a prelude to the resounding thud of its corpse. The barrel retreated and the panel quietly closed as the Order of the Guard secured the area.

Chapter Nineteen

After any incident, there was a debriefing, a moment for all involved parties to tell their accounts and make sense of things that happened in the blink of an eye. Aren mounted a full investigation once the remains of the groue horror were examined. They found what remained of the slain squad and traced Emer's movements preceding his transformation. Three squads escorted Chandi through Emer's ruin patrols over the past forty-eight hours in hopes that her presence would cleanse the area of any last drop of radiation that remained. In retrospect, it was rather easy to connect the dots but hindsight came at a cost.

When Chandi was called to give account of her actions, she stuck to the facts: who, what, where, when. When asked why she broke from the sept, Chandi could only answer truthfully: it seemed the right thing to do. Amongst the other students, reactions were mixed. There was newfound respect in some sentients' eyes, as the height of the monastery walls grew with each retelling. Some approved of her daring-do and chalked it up to bravery and fidelity to the sept, neither of which was strictly canon in the Church of Parkour but held popular appeal, even within the confines of monastic life. Others thought it was foolishness—when Netu yells "run," you run. Her closest friends were just glad she was alive and relatively uninjured. Even Moonstone seemed sympathetic and gave her a few dreamless nights.

It was a full moon tonight. Chandi never missed the chance to bask in the full moon; it was part and parcel of her remembrance. She was a child of moon, named in its brilliance and blessed in its light. She touched her mother's pendent. This was the first full moon she bore Moonstone since the night they first became acquainted. She recalled her awe when it shone in her hand, and now she didn't even want to hold it. She wanted to talk to it, know why it only glowed for her, ask it what it wanted from her. She wanted to know its price for freedom. And then there was Yan. They weren't exactly friends, but they were inextricably linked by an extraordinary event, and Chandi felt like she should visit. That seemed like the right thing to do, even if she couldn't enunciate the exact reason.

At first, she was too busy giving her account and clearing the ruins. The nature of Yan's injuries were not toxic in nature, so Chandi hadn't been called to serve. But the longer she stalled visiting, the harder it got to break inertia. Chandi wasn't sure what to expect. What do you say to someone whose life you saved? Was it fair to expect anything at all when they are still figuring out what it means to escape death's grasp?

When Chandi finally ran out of excuses, she made her

way to the infirmary and took a seat beside Yan's bed. The petite Asian pathfinder was lying on her side, curled in a fetal position. Chandi noted Yan's tear-streaked face and pillow; had they been close, she would have joked about what an ugly crier Yan was, but Chandi made no comment.

"What do you want?" Yan eventually choked out.

"I wanted to see how you were doing." It sounded lame, even to Chandi.

"I'm still here, thanks to you," Yan replied with more than a little disdain. "You should have let it get me."

"You don't mean that, Yan—"

"Don't tell me what I mean!" Chandi was stunned into silence; Yan had always been so calm and collected. "If I had run fast enough, I would have made it. If I hadn't, I would have escaped this unworthy vessel. I could have reincarnated into a better one." Her small frame shook with conviction.

"Do you want me to go?" Chandi asked in a quiet voice.

"I don't care what you do," Yan answered.

Chandi walked back to her room, dazed by Yan's chastisement. Lucy knew something was wrong as soon as Chandi opened the door, but waited for her to come it in her own time.

"How was Yan?" Lucy feigned the levity of polite conversation.

"Did you know she was a true believer?" Chandi inquired incredulously.

"Really?! Like 'if only we had run faster, we would have escaped the apocalypse and reincarnation under the shattered moon' true believer? I thought those were just stories theologians told kids to get them to run faster."

"Well, apparently it's a real thing." Chandi huffed as she kicked off her shoes and poured fresh water in the basin to wash her face. "It's not like I expected her to grovel and dedicate herself to repaying a life debt, but 'you should have let it get me' was not even on my radar," Chandi shamelessly mimicked the other pathfinder.

"She said that?"

"Yeah, like I robbed her of the opportunity of being reincarnated into a faster runner," Chandi punctuated words between splashes of water.

Lucy shook her head. "That is hardcore true believer."

Chandi changed into her nightclothes, careful to transfer Moonstone with it. "Did I tell you she yelled at me?"

"Yan raised her voice?" That did surprise Lucy. She lowered her head from the top bunk. "So I guess Yan isn't vying for my position as your best friend anytime soon?"

Chandi laughed. "I think you're safe."

Lucy blew out her light. "For what it's worth, if there is a monster chasing me and you distract it so I can run away, I won't yell at you for it."

Chandi smiled. Lucy always knew just what to say.

*****

Jackson was a little surprised to receive the abbess's summons and was relieved that for once, the commotion wasn't otherworldly in nature. He knocked on the solid wooden door, only to find it wasn't completely closed. Khiri was pacing and a swift wave of her hand led him to a nearby chair next to Brother Bartholomew. *So this is a caucus*, Jackson thought to himself as he closed the door and took a seat.

Khiri's robes rippled as she turned to address her brothers of the stride. The abbess got straight to the point. "In your professional opinions, could Moonstone be causing all this?"

Brother Bartholomew opened and closed his mouth no less than three times before offering a noncommittal, "Possibly?"

Jackson shrugged. "I'm no expert on lunar meteorites, but I've heard of crazier theories."

The tigress took a seat at her desk. "The elder council will assist us, but the soonest we can get a containment vessel is six months."

"Cassie can't shave a little more time off that?" Jackson piped up.

Khiri gave him a knowing look. "Do you think Cassie would wait a second longer than necessary to get her hands on Moonstone?" Jackson nodded. It was a fair point. "But there may be another way to remove Moonstone's presence from Unseen Waters sooner than that, if it is causing undo trouble to the monastery. There are stakes I'd rather not risk if both of you think Moonstone is of no consequence to the matter of the groue horror." Jackson's eyebrow rose at the nomenclature. "It's what the Inquisitives handling the dissection call the creature," the abbess explained to the sorcerer.

Brother Bartholomew lit his pipe—a necessity when pondering high thoughts. "There is no doubt that Moonstone can affect things from a distance."

"Chandi thinks it may be trying to communicate with her, even though she isn't a sorcerer," Jackson confessed. "But I can't honestly say I've heard of spiritual beings introducing monsters or toxins into the ruins that weren't firmly rooted in the otherworld first."

"Before Moonstone, you hadn't heard of a rock acting as a conduit to the moon, either," the owl pointed out.

"So what's at risk in Cassie's latest scheme?" Jackson queried.

Khiri didn't bother to suppress her smirk; he knew Cassie's capricious nature better than anyone. "She proposes Chandi drop Moonstone off at a nearby politically expedient location far enough away from the monastery that it shouldn't cause us any problems." Both brothers of the stride read between the lines.

"And the catch?"

"It involves unsanctioned running in unchartered ruins at night." Bartholomew balked while Jackson laughed—leave it to

Cassie to wish for the moon, even in its fractured state. "Initially, I dismissed the idea outright," Khiri added defensively. "But if this is no coincidence, I'm reconsidering my stance, provided that Cassie could provide enough resources to minimize risks."

"What's Cassie offering?" Jackson was curious how badly she and the elder council wanted this.

"Transport to and from unsanctioned lands and running Chandi with a sept of tracers."

Jackson whistled. "Whatever those old coots have in mind, it's something big." The resident scholar muttered something derisive about administration and bean counters under his breath.

"Cassie thinks I should let Chandi make the choice to run or not," Khiri added for Jackson's benefit. They both knew what a sore spot that was for her.

"Chandi's just a kid," Jackson dismissed.

"Here I must differ with you." Brother Bartholomew's brow ruffled. "Chandi is wiser than her years in some regards, and I think if the choice is presented in a neutral way, she could make an honest assessment on her own terms." He puffed his pipe once more. "And there is no question regarding her abilities. That 'kid' outran a groue horror, tic-tacked up a twenty-foot-tall wall, and dove off the other side without injury. Certain aspects of her training may need to be pushed up, but I've never known her to shirk from a challenge."

The sweet smell of the pipe tobacco lingered in the air

while the abbess took their council and reluctantly made her decision.

*****

The crisp evening air whipped around Chandi's face as she set the pace for the sept. Hemmed in on all sides by tracers, the pathfinder was certain that this was quite literally the coolest thing she had ever done; her only regret was that she couldn't tell Lucy about it. When the abbess called her into her office, Chandi knew she was supposed to seriously consider the dangers and risks, but all she could think about was running with tracers in unchartered territory at night. Yes, please, and thank you.

And then there was Moonstone. Chandi would have carried it for six months if necessary, but she would be lying if she said she was sad to part from its company. The cumulative weight of keeping it secret from Lucy alone was taxing, but it was more than that. What she once regarded as a good luck charm had become an albatross around her neck. It was becoming increasingly obvious to Chandi that their paths were at odds and neither could be happy until they were free of each other, regardless of the strength of their apparent connection. Once they parted ways, they would each be free to seek their true direction, and Chandi was looking forward to more blissful dreamless nights once she deposited the lunar meteorite in the ruins.

With a motion of her hand, the leader shifted the sept to the southwest, following the edge of the lake. The moonlight poked through clusters of clouds, granting Chandi enough light to marvel at the tracers' seamless transition; she felt clumsy in comparison even though she knew she was holding her own. They slowed as they neared the river and the designated drop-off point. Chandi opened the pouch Jackson had given her to carry Moonstone safely. A beam of moonlight pierced through a break in the cloud cover and the meteor glowed in her hand, as if to say farewell. Chandi silently wished Moonstone stillness, although she doubted such serenity lay in its future. Chandi dropped the stone amongst the rubble, its emanating light fading the second it left her hand.

There was nothing left to do but turn around and run into the night.

THE END

Chandi will next appear in *Chandi and the Pearl of Making*